FOUR CORNERS
DARK

William McNally

ISBN: 1463561857
ISBN 13: 9781463561857

CONTENTS

ENGINE 18

CHAPTER ONE

Anna Sanchez kneeled and crossed herself, and prayed to the Virgin of Guadalupe for protection. The old church echoed with the murmured prayers of her fellow travelers. She watched them huddled near the altar where one woman stared at pills in her hand. The man called Omar had given them birth control in case they were raped during the three-day trip through the Sonoran desert. Anna had thrown them away. Her late grandfather, a former boxer, had taught her to take care of herself.

There was a surge of activity and the crowd of people, loaded with backpacks and luggage, moved towards the front doors. They were waiting for the truck to the border town of Sasabe.

"It is time to leave," Omar shouted at the travelers.

Omar was not Mexican but spoke perfect Spanish. He appeared polite and professional, but Anna sensed a coiled snake behind his dark eyes. She followed the others to a 1960s-era farm truck with wood slates lining the open bed. The faded rust-colored paint peeled off in sections. She handed Omar her payment, climbed onto the back of the truck, and sat between two older women.

"Perdón," she said, sliding down between them.

She placed her knapsack on her lap and felt the cold metal of a revolver tucked in her jeans. The truck rumbled to life and started down the dirt road to Sasabe. The truck had a stenciled number thirteen painted on its windshield to enable the town to track the fees due it for allowing the service within its borders. Number thirteen picked up speed and delivered more souls to the dark desert, driving with lights off as the route was popular with bandits looking to rob the unfortunates who travelled it. Omar glanced out the dusty back window of the cab with a satisfied look on his face. Thirty-five heads was a good take for him tonight.

Anna's neighbors had told her about Omar, they called him a coyote, a smuggler who could bring people across the border to California in time for harvest. The price wasn't negotiable, one hundred dollars to Sasabe and two thousand to California. He promised a high success rate but no one really knew for sure, the people he smuggled never returned.

Anna planned to travel up the California coast working the strawberry and blackberry harvests. She had grown up using her hands and didn't mind the work. After the summer, she would go north to Redding where her aunt owned a bakery. Earlier in the week she had wired seventeen thousand dollars to her aunt, enough money to start a new life. In seventy-two hours she would be past the desert and free.

The moon was nearly full and cast a blue glow on the faces of the people huddled on the truck. There were families, a dozen or so younger people and the two older women next to her. Many were loaded with clothing and possessions. Anna carried only her knapsack and wore two sets of clothes. The only possessions she valued were the Colt stuck down the front of her jeans and the forged passport stuck somewhere else. Somewhere no one would find it. She remembered Omar's cold advice to the women.

"Take the pills," he had said. "You don't want to get to America knocked up. You can't pick knocked up."

She turned to one of the women next to her.

"Hello," she said to the woman.

"Hello. My name is Rosa," The old woman answered. Her teeth were brown stumps and her face was lined with years of misery. A faded tear drop was tattooed under her eye. "My son is waiting for me," she told Anna. "He is very successful in the United States and arranged for me to cross. I have waited so long to meet his family."

The old woman began to cry and Anna put an arm around her frail shoulder. The landscape sped by in shadows for several hours until the yellow lights of Sasabe appeared in the distance. The truck slowed and then came to a stop. The travelers sat waiting for the next step in their journey. Omar climbed out of the cab, looked around, and then opened the wooden tail gate.

"It's time. Get out," he yelled in Spanish. Anna and the others never saw the driver.

She climbed down from the back of the truck and then helped Rosa. The travelers were busy organizing their loads. Omar separated them into two groups and Anna was placed with the younger people, Rosa was placed with the others.

CHAPTER TWO

Omar walked out into the desert and disappeared from view. An hour passed, then another. People began to whisper to one another.

"Maybe we have been tricked," one woman said.

The truck and unseen driver were long gone. The two groups stood together shielded by a thicket of mesquite. Finally, Omar flashed the signal light for Anna's group to join him. They scurried across the desert scanning the moonlit ground for snakes and scorpions. When they reached him he signaled for the second group.

"Silence!" Omar hissed at two men whispering.

The second group was slower than the first, stopping to pick up items dropped along the way. Anna saw Rosa in the rear of the group struggling to carry her suitcase. She stepped forward to help, but was jerked backwards.

"You need to stay here," Omar said flatly. "They must come on their own."

Omar led them further into the desert. He walked easily across the difficult terrain avoiding obstacles while the others stumbled blindly behind him. The two groups had spread out considerably by the time they reached the halfway point. The distance was taking a toll on the old and the overloaded.

One of the women from the second group ran up to Omar. She was out of breath and dropped two bags both sprayed-painted black to help avoid detection.

"My husband has fallen and is badly hurt," she said. Omar stopped and stared at the woman.

"Where is he?" he asked blandly.

She gestured for Omar to follow her back along the line of travelers. Anna followed behind them. Omar and the woman reached the end of the line and found a middle-aged man groaning in pain. His leg was bleeding and a sharp white bone pierced his skin. Anna found Rosa towards the back still struggling with her suitcase.

Anna said, "Give it to me. I will carry it for you."

"Bless you," Rosa said. "Bless you."

Anna moved closer behind Omar and watched. The injured man lay in a pile of clothing, books and papers he had dropped when he fell.

Omar turned to the injured man's wife and said, "Take what you need from him. We are leaving."

"No!" she wailed. "We gave you everything we had. You promised to help us cross over."

"This is true," Omar said with a grin.

He pulled a Luger fitted with a silencer from his vest, aimed the gun and shot the man in the head. The man tumbled forward onto his belongings. His blood pooled in the sand like motor oil. The man's wife collapsed next to him and began to scream. Omar grabbed her by the hair and put the hot barrel of the gun into her mouth. She struggled, eyes wild, as he slid the long barrel down her throat causing her to gag.

"That's enough!" Anna said cocking the hammer of the Colt.

Her gun was aimed at the small of Omar's back. He pulled the barrel from the woman's mouth and turned to face Anna.

Smiling, he said, "She needs to decide if she wants to crossover with him or with us."

"She's coming with us," Anna said now aiming the gun at Omar's chest.

"Of course," he answered. "She will get what she deserves. Allow me."

Omar extended his hand towards Rosa's suitcase.

"No," Anna answered.

"Very well," Omar said.

He walked towards the front of the line and disappeared into the dark. People helped the distraught woman collect her belongings. She clung to her husband's body, but they implored her to leave.

"You cannot stay lady. The wolves will come," one man said.

"You must leave him. He is with god now," said another.

The group of travelers in the front started moving again. The woman, in tears, left her husband and moved on with her group. Anna stayed in the back, walking beside Rosa.

After an hours walk they reached a guarded crossing and Omar trained a pair of night vision binoculars on the road ahead. Portable observation towers dotted the horizon and unseen sensors ran along the border. He put down the binoculars, walked off to the side and spoke into a radio. When he finished his muted conversation, he holstered the radio and returned to address them.

"We need to continue west," he said flatly. "The security is too strong here. I have arranged for a train to take us across the border. There is a depot halfway to El Bajito. Of course, there will be a small additional cost to cover the expense."

"How much more?" a woman asked.

"We must hurry if we are to make the train. We can discuss payment when we arrive."

The exhausted travelers continued westward into the Pozo Verde Mountains, each step became more difficult as they climbed the rocky trail towards El Bajito. Some of the people whispered about turning back, afraid they would suffer the same fate as the man with the broken leg, but the fear of facing the desert alone stopped any defections.

Omar maintained a brutal pace as they walked through the night and the urgency in his stride told them they would be left if they fell behind. Anna walked behind Rosa who had surprising endurance forged from a life of hard labor. Excited whispers filtered through the line when someone spotted a light, but their relief turned to terror when they realized it was an approaching vehicle. Omar gestured for them to be quiet and stepped forward towards the light.

A pickup truck raced towards Omar and slid sideways, stopping just a few feet in front of him. The truck was painted a dark camouflage and modified with large tires on black rims. A 50-caliber machine gun was mounted in the bed of the truck. One man trained the gun on Omar while another shined a spotlight in his face. Omar stood relaxed in the glare of the light with his hands clasped in front of him.

"You are trespassing," the man with the spotlight said. He wore a black and green bandana and smoked a cigarette.

"Are you sure of that, my friend?" Omar asked calmly. He turned and stared into the eyes of the man on the machine gun.

"Am I what?" the man shouted back. "Do you know who we are?"

"Of course I do, Miguel," Omar answered. "I know you all very well, but the question is how well do you know Francisco?" Omar gestured towards the man behind the machine gun.

Miguel looked back and bullets began ripping through the cab. Francisco fired four hundred rounds leaving the truck oozing with bloody pulp and the bed filled with shell casings. Francisco sat dazed for a moment, then pulled a knife from his boot and plunged it into his own throat. Blood sprayed and sizzled on the hot metal of the gun barrel. Omar turned towards the travelers and found them all face down on the ground.

Anna had her Colt in her hand ready to fire. She put the gun away and helped Rosa to her feet.

"Let's move out," he said. His voice was matter of fact, as if he had just stopped to swat a fly.

CHAPTER THREE

The travelers were near the point of exhaustion when a brilliant light illuminated the clear desert sky. They followed Omar to a clearing where the outline of a magnificent train depot came into view. The building rose out of the desert sand six stories high. The roof capped two towers connected to a clock in the center of the building. The clock, which had no hands, was two stories high with Roman numerals on its face.

"We are here at last!" one of the women exclaimed.

Anna helped Rosa to the station fighting a sense of dread that trumped her fear of narcos and the border patrol. When they reached the building, people poured through etched glass doors and onto a balcony that overlooked the station floor. A single set of tracks ran along the far wall of the building and marble staircases led down to the platform. The station appeared to be empty with suitcases, water bottles and articles of clothing littering the polished floors.

The travelers, tired and filthy from the journey, followed Omar to the floor of the station. He was still perfectly groomed with polished boots and a crisply pressed shirt. He assembled them at the edge of the track.

"Group one, over here," he said, gesturing. "Group two, over there," he said, pointing down the platform.

Once the groups were in place he inspected and counted them.

"Thirty four heads" Omar said to himself.

He stepped over a disgarded suitcase and took his place in between the two groups.

They had waited in silence for an hour when one of the men finally spoke.

"Señor. How much longer for the train?"

Omar glared at the man and walked past him. No one asked again. They waited three more hours sitting on the marble floor of the station.

Shortly before 3 a.m. a train whistle sounded in the distance. When the whistle blew a second time the black hulk of a locomotive appeared in front of them followed by a coal car, an ornate rail car and twenty box cars. Engine 18 was stenciled in script on its side. The track underneath the train was in flames with hot embers between the smoldering ties.

The crowd stepped back as flames erupted from the train and spread throughout the station. The travelers were surrounded and began to scream. Anna and Rosa, in the back of the crowd, were knocked to the ground. They watched the flames engulf the travelers.

Anna helped Rosa take cover behind a bench. The fire swept across the platform and the travelers disappeared in waves of billowing smoke. Moments later they appeared in the barred windows of the box cars, shouting and pounding on the wooden doors.

Anna and Rosa were surrounded by fire and began to cough from the smoke. Anna spotted a gap in the flames and pulled Rosa towards the opening. A dark shape formed within the smoke and Omar stepped forward.

"Ladies?" he said politely, extending his hand.

"Stay where you are," Anna said pointing the Colt at Omar.

"As you wish," Omar responded.

Anna cocked the gun and fired a round past Omar's ear.

"We want out of here," she said.

"Of course," he said. Steam blew from his lips and caught Anna and Rosa in its scalding embrace.

CHAPTER FOUR

Anna woke staring at the ornate ceiling of a Pullman car. She was dazed, unable to focus her eyes and her right hand throbbed in pain. Her weapon was gone but an imprint of the gun was branded into her palm. Her grandfather had left the pistol and twenty thousand dollars to her father but he died before he could drink up the money. The police believed he was caught skimming collections from his employers, but Anna knew the truth. He came home drunk one night, began beating her, and she shot him.

Anna sat up and looked around the room. The walls were covered in satin walnut and polished to a brilliant shine. She tried to stand but collapsed back down in the chair.

"Don't try to stand yet. It will pass," someone whispered.

Three women she had been travelling with were in the room all dressed in an odd variety of clothing, one in a gown, another in a Roman tunic and the third in a leather bondage outfit.

The women looked drugged. Anna stood and approached a mirror hanging on the wall and saw a reflection she hardly recognized. She was dressed in a Nazi uniform. She turned towards the other women.

"Where the hell are we?" she asked.

"On a train," the woman in the bondage outfit shouted and began to laugh. She took a large gulp from a silver cup. "You should try this it is delicious," she said in a slurred voice.

A wine decanter full of a deep-red liquid sat on a table covered with white linen. Anna lifted the decanter and smelled the liquid, recoiling from the pungent smell. She put the decanter down in disgust.

"Where are the others?" she demanded.

"Back there," one of the women answered. "In the bad place." She giggled.

Anna walked to the back of the train car, swung open the door and stepped out on the observation deck where cold air whipped past her face. A mass of people writhed within the freight car behind her. The train was moving so fast that the landscape was indistinguishable. She needed to find Rosa and escape when it slowed. She walked back inside and found a doorway at the front of the car but the door was locked.

She peered through a stained glass window into the next room. Two young men were drinking from silver glasses and were dressed as oddly as the women. Anna knocked on the glass and the men waved and laughed.

She knocked again and pointed at the door. One of the men stumbled over and opened it. They were in a small office with a built-in mahogany desk and two burgundy leather chairs. The men saluted and began laughing as Anna walked past them.

CHAPTER FIVE

Anna entered a narrow passageway where a wood floor led to a series of doors. She pushed the first door inward. White bed linens were covered with blood and a silver cup had been dropped on the floor. Liquid had soaked into the wool carpeting and in the middle of the spill was a human finger. She put her hand to her mouth and stumbled back out into the passageway.

Somewhere ahead she heard Omar's voice. He spoke but she couldn't understand him, he wasn't speaking Spanish or English, but something else altogether. She walked to a door at the end of the passageway and listened. Cremo, acquire and piaculum, the language he spoke was Latin. She heard footsteps and slipped into another room; Omar walked past and addressed the women in the back.

"Ladies how are we doing?" Omar said. "More wine?" His voice had a festive ring.

She looked around the empty room, opened a closet door and found a silver cane hanging on a wooden peg. She took the cane and felt its weight. It was heavy, made from black ebony and silver. She gripped the cane, wincing from the pain in her hand, and waited to surprise Omar. He returned within a few minutes but wasn't alone.

"You will like it up here better than that box car," he said in Spanish. "But first I need you to do for me one small favor."

She peered out the door and saw one of the travelers walking behind Omar. He was an older man whose clothes were covered in soot and soaked with sweat. They walked into the next room.

Anna followed behind prepared to beat Omar to death. She swung open a door and entered a lavish dining room. The table was set with fine linens, crystal glasses and china. All the chairs surrounding the table were mahogany trimmed with red velvet, except the chair at the head of the table which was scorched black. She reached a door at the end of the train car and saw Omar and the man climbing down from the coal car and onto the locomotive.

Anna climbed onto the coal car, the wind whipped coal dust into her face as she crawled across the loose coal. She reached the end and peered over the edge, Omar was behind the man in the cab of the locomotive. The door of the firebox was open and the fire burned with blue-tipped flames. The man stared at the fire, dropped to his hands and knees then crawled into the firebox.

The man's screams rose above the wind as the fire engulfed him, then stopped leaving only the clacking of the train on the tracks.

Omar closed the door to the firebox, turned and suddenly appeared at the top of the coal car. Anna stumbled back and tightened her grip on the cane. He began to laugh and spoke in her father's drunken voice.

"Hija. You think you can ride for free and not pay for what you did to me?" he asked and began to laugh again.

Anna felt something wet soaking into the knees of her jeans. The bed of the car was no longer filled with coal but with bodies. She cried out and began crawling back towards the back of the train. She was covered in blood when reached the end of the car, and the cane slipped from her hand as she climbed down the ladder. Sparks flew as it ricocheted off of the tracks and disappeared into the night.

She jumped across to the Pullman car and fell onto the metal platform. Omar's silhouette was moving across the coal car towards her. She reached out and grabbed the pin that connected the train cars. She twisted the pin and it began to move, her burnt hand ached from the effort. She pulled harder and when the pin came free she lost her balance and tumbled onto the track between the cars. The locomotive and coal car roared ahead when the couplings disengaged and Omar smashed his fists and screamed in rage. His shadow turned from black to an orange flame then disappeared. The Pullman and its line of cargo cars slowly ground to a stop.

Anna saw a brilliant flash and awoke lying on the floor of the train depot. The ornate depot was a dilapidated shell, starlight streamed through holes in the ceiling, and the brick walls of the building were scorched and covered in soot. People were waking all around her. Some whimpered but most sat stunned staring in the dark. She climbed to her feet and walked to a far wall where she found Rosa.

"Gracias" Rosa said as Anna helped her up.

In the distance a train whistle echoed across the desert. Panicked voices began to rise in the depot. The whistle sounded again this time much closer. Anna grabbed Rosa and ran for the front doors of the building. They joined the other travelers and escaped into the desert night leaving their possessions behind scattered across the floor of the depot.

RETURN TO NOWHERE

CHAPTER ONE

September 1st, 1944. 9:01 a.m. The fog formed a dense blanket beneath the orange glow of the bridge. A cold mist infused the wind as cars sped by unaware of a man standing on the brink of death. The man moved quickly and deliberately oblivious to the cold or the cars. He was unlike others who had jumped from the Golden Gate. Frank Reynolds had jumped from this bridge before. Some did survive, battered and broken but Frank wouldn't take that chance again. He climbed onto the metal railing and held a steel cable for balance. The bed of fog below was twenty-five stories down and ended in granite hard water. He glanced at his watch, threw down his cigarette and jumped head first.

He fell into the sea of white fog and remembered the first time he jumped, soon after the bridge opened in 1937. He had taken a financial beating in '29 and lost everything, including his wife and kids. After struggling on for a few years he had reached the end of the line. The sky was a clear blue that day and the water was visible below him. He remembered the makes, models and license plate numbers of every car that passed by. Earlier that day a couple had stopped to ask him directions.

"Morning fella. Could you tell us the way to the Opal Hotel?" A blonde in the passenger seat asked.

The couple drove a black Packard One sedan, license plate California 8K4234. The woman smoked a cigarette and was quite attractive. The husband was flustered and impatient. They were up from Los Angeles on their honeymoon. Frank recalled the event, like every other moment in his life, with perfect clarity.

"Head over the bridge," Frank answered. "Take Doyle Drive to 1050 Van Ness. The Opal's on the left."

The woman turned to the man behind the wheel and said, "See why you stop and ask directions? We were heading the wrong way."

The man just shrugged and said, "Thanks buddy."

The moment they drove away he stepped off the new bridge feet first, hit the water and plunged twenty five feet deep. He broke both his legs on the bottom of the bay but didn't die until the salt water filled his lungs. That first pain-filled drowning taught him something important about himself. He couldn't really die.

CHAPTER TWO

August 31st, 1944. Frank Reynolds was now forty years old, single with few friends. He made his way through life playing cards and ran afoul of a gang called the Black Hand when he won too often. He changed clubs frequently but the reach of the gang had extended and it was impossible to find any action they didn't run. The Black Hand's vicious reputation extended as far as Chicago and it wasn't good for business to get taken by a shark. With a bounty on his head, Frank's days were numbered and he wasn't planning to find out what that number was.

"Morning Mister Reynolds," the receptionist said. "Please have a seat. Mr. Victor will be with you momentarily."

He took a seat in a polished mahogany chair and placed two leather satchels on either side. He felt the weight of a chrome revolver in the pocket of his jacket.

Charles Victor poked out of a glass door and exclaimed, "Mr. Reynolds, it is so nice to see you again. I am sorry to keep you waiting, please come in."

Frank walked into the office and sat across from Victor who managed the Village Bank & Trust.

"Is everything ready Charles?" Frank asked.

"Of course Mr. Reynolds. Per your instructions we have liquidated all of your assets," Victor answered.

Frank dropped the leather satchels on the desk.

"Would you care for a coffee or tea Mr. Reynolds?" Victor asked.

"No. I am in a bit of a hurry Charles. If you don't mind," Frank said gesturing towards the empty bags.

"Of course Mr. Reynolds." Charles Victor padded across the lush carpeting of his office and began spinning the tumbler of a wall safe.

Seven, five, zero, Frank knew the combination. Over the years he had observed Victor opening the safe dozens of times, glimpsed the turns and committed the combination to memory.

"When will we see you again Mr. Reynolds? Soon I hope," Victor asked.

"Could be a while this time," Frank answered.

Victor placed a bank bag on his desk and sat down. "Here you are Mr. Reynolds. Three hundred and sixty thousand dollars in cash with an equal amount moved to your safety deposit box."

Charles Victor watched in amazement as Frank Reynolds stood and walked out the door carrying a small fortune.

Frank climbed into a Buick coupe and drove north to an isolated point along the Pacific Ocean. The clouds obscured the sun creating a blue haze as the relentless ocean surged against the shoreline. He opened the truck, retrieved a length of rope then climbed down to a ledge and hid the bags in a narrow gap in the rock face. He climbed back up and sat on the bumper of the car and smoked a Chesterfield, holding the cigarette between his lips while he untied the rope.

Frank drove back into San Francisco and onto the bridge. He got out of the car, climbed the retaining wall and jumped into the Pacific. For the second time, Frank returned to nowhere, the place before birth and the place after death, where he couldn't remember anything.

CHAPTER THREE

September 1st, 1944. 9:02 a.m. Frank regained consciousness in Chicago, Illinois, moments after he stepped off the bridge. He was now Frank Reynolds ESQ, a Chicago attorney with a wife named Winifred. At first his memories were a blur, a combination of old and new lives.

"Frank, are you okay?" his wife Winnie asked.

She had a frightened look in her eyes and had asked that question many times over the past weeks. Finally his confusion subsided and the cigarette-smoking, card playing Frank was back. He left only questions from friends and family when he walked out the door and drove to the Chicago Union Station.

"How much for a ticket to San Francisco? First class," Frank asked.

The ticket agent peered at him through thick spectacles.

"Round trip or one way?" the agent asked.

"One way. Make it a roomette," Frank answered.

"One hundred and twenty-six dollars and eleven cents please," the ticket agent said.

Frank slapped down one hundred and thirty dollars. "When does it leave?" he asked.

"Twelve forty-five sir."

Frank looked at his gold pocket watch. He had twenty minutes.

The agent handed Frank his change and his ticket and said, "Safe travels sir."

He turned and walked towards a glimmering streamliner. In fifty hours he would be back on the West Coast and with any luck, have recovered some or all of his money. It all depended on how events had changed in this new life. When he jumped he entered another possible path in the life of Frank Reynolds. This time it was a path where he had excelled at school, attended church and never run into the Black Hand Gang.

He handed his ticket to the blue-suited conductor and climbed aboard the train.

"Have a safe journey sir," the man said.

"Thanks pal," Frank replied.

The trip to San Francisco was uneventful. He slept and read for the greater part of it and smoked on the observation deck when no one else was around. On the second day, he walked the aisles of the train cars and studied the passengers along the way, businessmen in suits, old women travelling to visit family and soldiers on leave.

He had met many people over the years but didn't have much use for them. They were passing scenery. His first jump in '37 had changed and disconnected him. He lived a disposable life in a disposable world. The whistle blew and the train began to slow as it approached the San Francisco station. A few minutes later, Frank hotwired a grey Ford and drove out of the station parking lot towards the point.

When he arrived he pulled the Ford to a stop in the same spot as the Buick, months earlier.

A section of the rock wall had crumbled into the sea. He was able to hike down and reach the hiding spot, but his bags were gone.

"Son of a bitch," Frank yelled.

He lit a cigarette and stared at the ocean.

"Should have buried it," he muttered.

He finished the cigarette and stamped it out in the dirt. He got into the car, put the column shifter in gear and gunned the accelerator leaving a cloud of dust behind him.

CHAPTER FOUR

The drive through Pacific Heights had an odd feel and all of his old haunts were gone. Tommy's Tavern was shuttered up and the building that held the Seville Club was gone completely, only an empty lot remained. Frank's stomach began to knot up when he approached his old neighborhood. He pulled up and parked in front of his house. The white trim of the hundred-year-old Queen Anne mansion stood against familiar blue paint but the grounds looked different. The oak tree was gone replaced by a swatch of ivy and a marble fountain.

A woman opened the front door of the house, stepped onto the front porch and left two empty bottles in a metal milk box. He pulled out a cigarette, crumbled the empty package and threw it into the back seat. After waiting a few minutes, he got out of the car and walked around the house to the back garden. He saw the woman through the kitchen window. She was young and pretty and looked to be in her mid-twenties. The kitchen was painted a different color and the house had windows where there hadn't been any before.

He peered over a wrought iron fence then opened a gate into the back gardens. The gate hinges made a low groan as it swung inwards. He walked into the yard and stopped in front of a glass greenhouse. The building was two stories high and attached to the back of the house. A mass of plants grew behind the translucent walls. The building had been built over the spot where Frank had hidden the key to his safety deposit box.

"Dammit," Frank said and threw down the remains of his cigarette.

He returned to the Ford and drove towards the ocean to consider his options. He was good for cash at the moment but needed a new plan. The key would not be under the greenhouse. The money, the safety deposit box or even the bank itself might not exist on this new path. He got a room at the Regal Hotel and then went outside to get some air. He saw a familiar face, Stewey Johnson, a grifter he had hired on occasion. Stewey was standing on the sidewalk with his hands in his pockets.

"Stewey, is that you?" Frank said with his hand out.

Stewey didn't recognize Frank and had a perplexed look on his face. It was a look Stewey often had so it was difficult to tell when he was really perplexed.

"Do I know you mister?" Stewey asked.

"Stewey are you wacky? It's me Frank. I'm a friend of Al's," Frank said.

"Oh yeah," Stewey said hesitantly. "I think I remember you. My head's not so good these days."

"You and me both," Frank said.

Clenching a cigarette between his teeth, Frank pulled out a roll of cash and Stewey's eyes lit up.

"I need a piece, can you help me out?" Frank asked.

Stewey glanced around and then pulled out a black revolver. He handed the gun to Frank. "Watch out, it's loaded," Stewey said.

"How much?" Frank asked.

"Three saw bucks."

Frank slapped thirty dollars into Stewey's hand.

"See you around Stewey," Frank said. He now had a plan.

CHAPTER FIVE

December 1st, 1944. Frank sat alone at the counter of Petey's Diner. The clock on the wall read 9:34 a.m. He threw his napkin on his half eaten food and paid his tab.

"Come back and see us," said his waitress.

"Sure," Frank lied, then tipped his hat and left.

He walked down the street towards the Village Bank & Trust and hoped like hell it still existed. A newspaper flew across the street blown by the wind. Morning commuters were busy rushing through the city streets. Frank buttoned his gray overcoat against the cold and ducked into a doorway to light a cigarette. He stepped back onto the sidewalk and let out a puff of smoke. The bank building was one block ahead. He was relieved seeing the bank, but still nervous. What if Victor doesn't recognize him? What if the cash is gone?

Never there in the first place? All was possible on this new path.

He stubbed out his cigarette and walked through the revolving door into the marble lobby and spotted a familiar face at a small, mahogany desk.

"Miss Talbot, you look well," Frank said.

A woman with grey hair tucked neatly in a bun glanced up at Frank with a stunned look on her face.

"Mr. Reynolds," she responded. Her voice was weak.

The relief washed over Frank. She knew him here and that was a good thing.

"Is Charles available?" Frank inquired.

The look on her face alarmed Frank.

"Mr. Reynolds, Mr. Victor is dead," she answered.

"What happened?" Frank asked.

She spoke hesitantly. "We were robbed. Mr. Victor was shot during a robbery."

The tone of her voice indicated surprise that he didn't know this had happened. He sat down in the chair next to her with his mind reeling.

Suddenly tires screeched outside the bank and four policemen burst into the lobby with their guns drawn.

Miss Talbot shouted, "Over here. He's here."

Frank whirled around the desk and grabbed her. He pulled the gun out of his coat pocket and aimed the pistol at her head.

"What the hell is going on?" he asked.

The policeman advanced with their guns trained on Frank. He backed into the bank offices with his left arm wrapped around Miss Talbot's throat.

"Back off you're making a mistake," Frank shouted at the policeman.

He pulled the woman into Charles Victor's empty office and spun to face her.

"Why did you call them?"

"Because you killed Mr. Victor," she said pointing at a leather chair with a half dozen holes shot through it.

"Why would I kill Charles?" Frank stammered.

Miss Talbot was shaking violently now. "Because you said he should have your money. He didn't know what you were taking about. You only had a small sum in this bank."

"When was the robbery?" Frank asked.

"Three months ago. September 1st," she answered.

That was the date of his last jump. He had been a gambler and worse over the years but had never killed anyone. Glass shattered and tear gas canisters rolled onto the floor. He left Miss Talbot coughing in the office and ran to the back of the building.

Years before, Charles Victor had shown him a secret apartment built for the founder of the bank. He searched for the entrance and located a small spiral staircase hidden behind marble columns. He climbed the stairs to the apartment then slipped in the door and locked it behind him.

The furniture in the rooms was covered in white sheets and the air was stale. He found a window and squeezed through it onto a ledge. Police sirens wailed in front of the bank. He was able to jump onto the roof of a hotel next door and ran down a set of stairs into the building. He found an elevator and pushed the call button. The lift arrived and he was greeted by a smiling operator in a black suit.

"What floor sir?" the operator asked.

"Lobby." Frank answered. "What's all the commotion outside?"

"The bank's been robbed again," the man answered. "Second time this year. Last time a fella got both his legs shot off. They sent him to Alcatraz for life."

The elevator bell rang when they reached the lobby. Frank walked through the hotel lobby and exited, glancing at the roadblock in front of the bank. Police were swarming everywhere and a crowd had gathered to watch. He walked around the corner and found the Ford parked along the curb. He pulled a parking ticket from under the windshield and climbed behind the wheel of the Ford, lit a cigarette and flinched as a police car raced past him. Once again things had become unmanageable. He turned onto Lombard Street and headed back to the bridge.

Frank stared over the edge of the bridge, the wind whipped past the cables buffeting him as he held on. He finished his cigarette, climbed up on the wall and jumped head first. The wind blew him into a cement pier and he tumbled into the bay.

Moments later he regained consciousness. The air was cold and damp and all around him were gray shadows. Seagulls cried and the air smelled of the sea. He sat up and tumbled onto a stone floor. Pain shot through his body. His eyes adjusted to the darkness and he realized he was in a prison cell. He reached for his legs but found only bandaged stumps. Suddenly Frank remembered everything, killing Charles Victor, the machine gun bullets and the life sentence. Beyond the cell window the bridge floated in an endless fog.

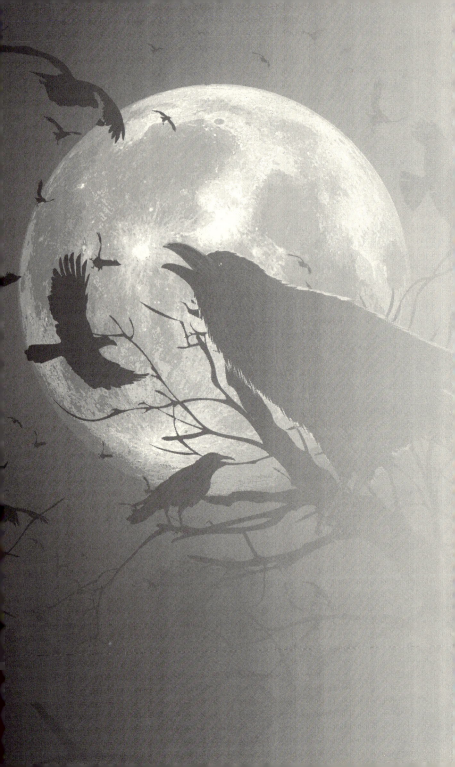

THE RAVEN MOCKER

CHAPTER ONE

Terry James navigated the steep incline of the gravel driveway. The lodge loomed through ancient oaks with only moonlight illuminating the hulking shape of the building. He parked his truck in the circular drive and glanced over at his sleeping wife. The stress of the last two months had taken a toll on her. The loss of her sister in a car accident followed by a move from Denver to the Blue Ridge Mountains. He climbed out and tried not to wake her.

His uncle Ted had left him the lodge and two hundred acres. The original structure had been a log building, but a collection of rooms had been added over the years. Ted had been an antiques dealer and travelled the world buying unusual pieces for private collectors.

He kept many items for himself stored in this rustic palace.

Terry grabbed an armload of clothes and walked to the front door of the lodge then searched his pocket for the key his uncle's attorney had given him. He opened the door and stepped into the cool dark of the lodge. He pulled back curtains allowing the moonlight to spill through towering windows and then lit a fire to warm the room.

He walked back to the truck and found Abby in a daze having just woken up.

"Hey welcome home," he said. "Ready to see the place?"

"Sure," she answered with a yawn.

"What do you say we just bring in what we need for tonight?" Terry asked. "I can grab the rest in the morning."

She nodded and slowly stepped out of the truck then grabbed a suitcase from the back seat.

"This is all I need."

Terry took Abby's hand and led her down the path to the front door then stepped aside to let her enter.

"After you," he said with a sweeping gesture. "Keep in mind it is a little rough. Power should be on first thing in the morning."

She walked across the stone entryway to the fireplace. The glow of the fire illuminated the room and created shadows up to the high peaks of the ceiling.

"Wow," she said. "This place is huge."

"Well then you will love the rest of this place. There is a lot more to show you tomorrow," Terry said.

He lit a candle from the flames of the fire and led her upstairs to a bedroom.

"I'll bring up the sleeping bags from the truck," Terry said.

"Don't forget the pillows," she said sitting on the edge of an unmade bed.

The flickering light of the candle danced across the wooden planks of the ceiling.

"Back in a flash," Terry said.

Abby didn't answer. She had fallen asleep on the bed.

CHAPTER TWO

Terry woke to a sound he had not heard for many months, Abby's laughter.

"What's so funny?" Terry asked.

She was looking out the wide expanse of windows on the back wall of the bedroom.

"These two little ... ah I am not even sure what they were. They looked liked skinny little dogs. Were chasing each other all around the back garden," she replied. "Just when one would catch up to the other they would change direction and run the other way. They finally ran towards a river near the woods. Did you know there was a river?"

"No," Terry answered glancing out the window. "I've never been back there," he added.

"Well, I am ready for the tour now," Abby said with a smile.

They walked out of the room and onto a second floor landing.

"I'm surprised there are any trees left in that forest," she said gesturing at the timbers that made up the lodge's rafters.

"Yes," said Terry. "My uncle poured his heart and soul into this place. It started with an old Indian lodge which makes up the north side of the structure."

"Well let's check it out," Abby said.

"Where would you like to start?" Terry asked.

"Outside, maybe we will see those two animals again."

Terry led Abby through the house and down a set of steps to a garden behind the lodge.

"Let's start there," Abby said pointing towards a stone bridge crossing a river.

A path beyond the bridge led into the woods. The path was bordered with downed trees and small saplings.

"Okay," said Terry.

They crossed the bridge and walked the path for hours caught in the hypnotic power of the forest.

"Whoa, hold up a second," said Terry.

"How long have we been in here?"

"I ... don't know," said Abby. "I lost track myself."

Terry looked for the sun through the dense trees. The light was faint.

"We better get out of here, we don't want to be in here after dark," he said.

"How far do you think it is back to the lodge?" Abby asked.

"Not sure," said Terry. "But we better hurry."

They moved quickly along the darkening path as the woods around them began to change. Suddenly, Abby recoiled.

"It's the animals I saw playing by the river," she gasped.

Terry stepped in front of her and saw two dead coyotes hung from a tree branch.

"Who would do such a thing?" Abby shouted.

"Not sure. Poachers maybe," Terry replied. "But these couldn't be the same animals you saw this morning. They look like they've been dead for some time."

"But they are. I'm sure of it," Abby insisted.

"I'll take it up with the police in the morning," Terry said. "We better get out of these woods."

They emerged behind the lodge as the last rays of the sun shone through the leaves of the trees. Exhausted, they crossed the stone bridge that separated the forest from their new home.

CHAPTER THREE

The next morning Terry hopped into his truck to drive into town and noticed a man in his rear view mirror. He backed the truck up and spotted the man in the woods along the drive.

"Hey you there," Terry shouted climbing out of the Jeep.

An older man with waist-length white hair stepped out of the woods. He was Native American and carried wild flowers.

"You must be Terrence," said the man.

"I am," replied Terry. "And you are?"

"My name is Joseph Wood. I was a friend of your late uncle. The man paused for a moment looking at the flowers. I am sorry for your loss, he passed over too soon."

"Thank you Mr. Wood."

"Please call me Joseph," replied the man.

"Only my uncle called me Terrance," Terry said. "Call me Terry."

"Of course," said Joseph. "I was just stopping by to say hello. I live a few miles down Turner Road," Joseph said gesturing towards the road. "Out here that means we're next-door neighbors."

"I was heading into Silverton to run a few errands but they can wait," Terry said. "Come on up to the house for some coffee. My wife Abby would love to meet you," he added.

Joseph visited with Terry and Abby, drinking coffee and discussing local lore. He talked about Terry's Uncle with great respect and affection. After two cups of coffee he stood to leave.

"Well, thank you for the hospitality. I must be getting back," Joseph said.

"Joseph, thank you again for the flowers. They are beautiful," Abby said as she and Terry walked Joseph to the front door.

"I want you both to be happy here. There are wonderful things here, but also many things you need to understand," Joseph said.

"Like poachers?" Terry asked.

"I am not sure I follow you."

"We found two coyotes strung up in a tree," Terry said. "Out in the woods."

"How unfortunate," Joseph said. "But I doubt any poachers or anyone else would be in those woods. I better let you folks get back to what you were doing. I'm sure you have a lot of work to do."

Joseph walked down the drive and disappeared into the eastern woods.

CHAPTER FOUR

T erry pulled the truck into a parking space in front of Dobbins hardware store.

"Can you believe this place?" Abby said.

"Pretty quaint," Terry said. "I hope they take kindly to strangers."

Terry and Abby walked into the ancient hardware store. The store was filled with a bizarre array of items for sale, Coke bottles and old signs lined the walls. He picked up a triple-bladed cabbage cutter.

"This looks like a must have for the Silverton lady."

"I don't think so," Abby said.

A man wearing overalls walked around the aisle.

"Actually that's a top seller of ours. Ladies and men. You folks new around here?"

"Yes, we just moved here from Denver," Abby answered. "Sorry, my husband has a bad sense of humor."

"No problem. Name's Frank Reynolds. I run the place. Let me know if you need help finding something. I have plenty more of the cabbage cutters in the back," he said with a wink.

After leaving the hardware store, Terry and Abby strolled around the town square enjoying the warm day. They walked passed an old jailhouse, near which a pile of stones was visible in a small field.

"Interesting," Terry said. "Let's go have a look."

The pile contained thousands of small stones, many with names and symbols written on them.

A tarnished plaque was mounted over the pile.

Terry read the plaque aloud. "1823. This spot marks the grave of a Raven Mocker. The brave people of Silverton forced this witch's black soul into the place between life and death."

"Creepy," Abby said.

"Maybe we better add a few rocks to hold the old bat down," said Terry.

"Better watch your tongue," Abby said.

"Sorry, I meant hold the old raven down," Terry said. "No disrespect."

They returned to their truck, Frank Reynolds was locking the glass doors of his shop.

"You folks still out?" Frank asked.

"Yeah," Terry replied as he opened the door to the Cherokee. "Past our bedtime, we're heading home." Terry smiled half expecting a smack from Abby.

"Well, watch the roads at night here," Frank said. "They're as twisty as they are dark, and if you drive off one you'll be going down for a while."

Frank picked up a brown leather briefcase and started down the sidewalk in front of the store. "Night," Frank said.

"Goodnight Mr. Reynolds," Abby said warmly.

During the drive back home the sun danced off shimmering trees and the forest rolled like an endless carpet into the mountain range.

"Watch out," Abby screamed.

Terry slammed on the brakes and swerved around a large black bird in the middle of the road.

"Damn," Terry said.

"Remember what Mr. Reynolds said. We have to be careful around these roads," said Abby.

"From now on the birds better be careful," Terry grumbled.

"Let's stop at Joseph's house to invite him for dinner tomorrow night," Abby said. Joseph had mentioned he didn't have or want a phone.

"Sure."

Terry looked for the turn off to Joseph's place. He had told them it was marked by a stump with a dream catcher hung above it.

"There it is," Abby said. "Ahead on the left."

Terry turned the Jeep onto a narrow rutted drive and the vehicle rocked violently from side to side. The sun was setting behind the trees and the forest was growing dark. After two miles of rocking along the dirt road they spotted Joseph's cabin. Dozens of farm implements, tools, and pans hung from the front of the cabin and a single rocking chair sat on the weathered porch.

"No wonder he walks to our place," Terry said. "This road will cost you a set of tires each trip."

They got out of the Jeep and walked to the cabin. The rusted metal roof was covered with vines and the front door was constructed from sticks bound together with rope. The Jeeps lights flickered off leaving them in complete darkness.

"Abby wait here," Terry said groping his way off the porch.

He walked to the dark shape of the truck then opened the rear hatch and found a flashlight.

"Flashlight's dead," Terry called to Abby.

"I thought you changed the batteries before the trip."

"I did," Terry replied. "I also replaced the Jeep's battery. Look what good that did."

He dug into his front pocket and pulled out his cell phone which was also dead.

"Abby, try your phone," Terry said.

She rummaged through her bag. "No good. I left my phone at the lodge. But hey, grab the bag in the back seat. I bought some candles at the hardware store," she said. "There are matches in there as well."

Terry lit two large candles and walked back onto the porch. The vanilla scent of the candles was out of place with the mossy smell of the forest. He knocked on the log door.

"I don't think he's home," Terry said. "The place is completely dark."

"Where could he be on foot at this hour?" Abby said.

"Wait here a minute," Terry said as he walked towards the back of the cabin.

He approached a pond and the black water shimmered in the candle light. There was no sign of Joseph but he saw something slide off the end of the dock. He looked down into the water and saw Abby under the surface with her hands outstretched and a scream frozen on her face.

"Abby," Terry yelled and plunged into the cold water.

He hit the muddy bottom and searched the murky water.

"Abby," Terry yelled.

"Terry," Abby shouted in the distance.

"Where are you?" He yelled.

He was up to his neck in water with the candle floating next to him.

"I'm over here," Abby said emerging from the front of the cabin.

"What happened?" she asked, alarmed at the sight of him climbing out of the water.

"I thought I saw something in the water, I thought I saw you."

CHAPTER FIVE

The couple walked the road from Joseph's cabin to the lodge, stopping briefly at the Jeep to grab a blanket and the remaining candles. An hour later they arrived at the lodge.

"We better get you in front of a warm fire," Abby said.

Terry nodded and tried to stop shaking. He had removed his clothes and beaten them against a tree to dry them but they were still damp. The blanket wrapped around him was soaked and did little to stop his shivering. They walked in the front door of the lodge and found a fire roaring in the fireplace.

"What the hell!" Terry said. "Is someone here?"

Other than the crackling fire there was silence.

"Joseph, are you here?" Terry called out.

No response. Terry grabbed a fireplace poker and wielded it in front of him.

"I need to check the house. You better stay close," he said.

"Okay," Abby whispered.

"Abby? Do you still have that Mace?" Terry asked.

"Yes," she whispered opening her hand. She was already holding the spray.

They walked through the lodge and searched room by room for an intruder. The lodge was large and sprawling with close to thirty rooms in all. Terry opened the door to the pool room, the last place to be searched. The room was filled with Native American artifacts contrasted by a large ornate billiard table in the center of the room. Behind a cherry bar was a mirrored wall with a section open.

"Abby wait here," Terry said as he crossed the room towards the opening.

"Not a chance," she replied staying close behind.

He examined the opening in the mirror which led to a room behind it. A breeze blew out his candle when he stepped through the doorway.

"Damn," he said. "Hand me that oil lamp behind you."

Abby turned to find a lamp with an ornate base engraved with a ring of crows.

"Here," she said.

He lit the lamp and walked behind the mirror door. Abby followed a few feet behind. The room was lined with bows, rifles, and an old musket.

"Looks like a museum in here," Terry said.

In the far corner, the stone floor had an opening with a ladder sticking out of it. Terry reached for one of the guns but thought better of it. A missed shot with stone walls could cause a ricochet. And worse, he hadn't shot a gun in years.

"Abby can you wait here?" Terry asked.

She looked scared but nodded in agreement. He descended into the opening and reached the floor of a cavern, then walked to an elongated pool of water. He fell hard on the wet stone floor and smashed the lamp. In the dark a faint blue light emanated from the pool. Abby heard him fall then ran to the ladder where a cold hand slid up the back of her neck and grabbed her hair.

"No," she yelled then sprayed the Mace into the empty room.

"Terry," she yelled. "Where are you?"

"I'm coming up."

As Terry groped his way to the base of the ladder, a mist descended on him and his eyes began to burn.

"Oh shit," Terry said as he rubbed his burning eyes.

He stumbled in the dark towards the pool of water.

Abby called down to Terry. "Are you okay?" Her voice quivered with fright. "Answer me, please."

"I'm fine," he croaked from below, coughing from the suffocating spray. "Stay up there!"

He crawled towards the sound of the rushing water with his face burning and eyes sealed shut then felt the cool spray of the water and began splashing his face. The effects of the Mace vanished immediately. He stood, walked to the base of the ladder and climbed back up.

"What happened down there?" she asked.

"I found a cave and stream that glows."

"Someone grabbed the back of my hair," Abby said.

"What?"

"Yes. Someone grabbed me and when I turned around, they were gone."

Terry picked up an old rotary phone hanging on the wall.

"The line's dead," he said. "We better get over to the sheriff's office in the morning."

They walked back through the lodge carrying candles for light, when they entered the great room it was dark. Terry examined the fireplace and found it cold with a fresh set of unburned logs in the grate.

"How is this possible?" he said. "We weren't gone for long."

"My watched stopped," Abby said.

Terry checked his watch and both had stopped at 3:00 a.m. The grandfather clock in the great room was also silent.

"Terry, something's not right about this place," Abby said. "Didn't your uncle say anything?"

"No, he never mentioned anything out of the ordinary," Terry answered.

"We need to talk to Joseph and find out what is going on around here," Terry said. "But for now, we'd better get some sleep." He grabbed another poker from the fireplace.

CHAPTER SIX

Terry was startled awake when someone pounded on the front door. He looked out the side window of the bedroom and saw the sun shining off the hood of his Jeep. He walked down the log staircase and left Abby asleep upstairs. The great room was awash in the amber glow of the sun. Opening the front door, he found Joseph.

"Joseph, I'm glad to see you."

"Likewise," Joseph said. "May I come in?"

"Please," Terry said.

He followed Terry to the kitchen table and sat holding his hat on his lap.

"Terry, is Abby around?" Joseph asked. "I need to explain a few things to you both."

"Sure Joseph. Let me go check to see if she is up yet," Terry answered.

Terry walked into the great room and found Abby walking towards the kitchen.

"Good morning," Abby said.

"Good morning Abby. Do you both have a few minutes? I need to explain a few things to you both," Joseph said.

"Sure, we have questions for you," Abby answered.

Joseph and Abby sat at the kitchen table while Terry made coffee.

"Sometimes a place is much more than it appears on the surface," Joseph began. "Picture a lake, serene on the surface, with miles of caves underneath. The lake is beautiful, but also deadly. That is the way it is here. This lodge was built on a border between the living and the dead. Terry, your uncle understood this place and respected it, however something had changed in him recently and he lost site of the danger."

"Joseph," Terry said. "What exactly are you getting at?"

"I had hoped to have more time with you both, but changes are happening faster than I anticipated," Joseph answered. "This place is a fulcrum, a balancing point. Your uncle became compelled to test the power and limits of this balance. You will see wondrous things here but be careful to treat them like you would a venomous snake and avoid them whenever possible."

Joseph stood and walked around the great room and studied the multitude of artifacts hanging on the walls.

"Your uncle had a great deal of faith in you Terry," Joseph said. "He entrusted all of this to you." He gestured around the lodge. "He spent his life putting this place together and it meant a great deal to him. Well, I must be going. I have taken enough of your time."

"Please Joseph," Abby said, "join us for an early supper this evening. So we can talk some more."

"As you wish," Joseph said. "Thank you for the invitation." He stood and left.

"What in the world was that about? Can you believe that guy?" Terry asked exasperated.

"Be nice. Local legends can be very ingrained. They were the way people explained the unexplainable," Abby answered.

"Yeah, a hundred years ago," Terry replied.

"I suspect there's a natural phenomenon here that people label as supernatural," Abby said. "I find it interesting."

"Well, I am going into town to file a police report. Let's see if the sheriff finds it interesting."

"Good, let me give you a shopping list so you can stop at the store on the way back." Abby said. "We need supplies for tonight." She smiled and went to find a pad of paper.

CHAPTER SEVEN

Terry climbed into the Jeep, turned the key and the engine started right away. He drove cautiously on the twisty road into town and slowed as he caught a glimpse of a boy emerging from the woods. The boy wore ripped overalls and looked to be seventeen or eighteen. Terry was shocked when he saw his face. The kid looked like Daniel Carver, a former student. He pulled the truck over and fought to catch his breath, he had suffered from asthma since he was a kid. He found his inhaler in the glove box and sucked in a deep breath.

Two years ago, Terry had resigned his position as a math teacher and football coach for Springside High School. Daniel Carver had been one of his student players. On a hot spring day, Daniel succumbed to the heat and collapsed into a coma. Three days later, he was dead and Terry was in the middle of a firestorm of accusations. After three months of hell, Terry was cleared of any negligence and allowed to return to normal life. Only life was no longer normal for Terry at Springside. It was anything but normal. He muddled on for a while trying to put the tragedy behind him, when he received the call about his uncle's death. The news was sad, but it did offer an opportunity, he and Abby could start over again in a new place far from Springside.

After regaining his composure, Terry drove on to Silverton and arrived at the sheriff's station. He opened the glass door of the station and walked in.

Rita Haeckel, a plump redhead, sat behind a steel desk. "Can I help you?" She barely looked up from the fingernail painting that occupied her attention.

"Yes, I need to see the sheriff," Terry answered.

"Sorry, Sheriff Turner went out for coffee at Wyatt's. Round the corner past Dobbins Hardware. Better step on it mister," Rita said. "Sheriff goes straight out on his rounds after Wyatt's. Could be gone for a while after that."

"Thanks," Terry said leaving the station.

Terry walked to Wyatt's, then entered the old building and found a heavy-set policeman at the lunch counter eating pie and drinking a cup of coffee.

"Sheriff Turner?" Terry inquired.

"Yes sir, what can I do for you?"

"My name is Terry James. I recently moved into my uncle's lodge."

"I know who you are Mister James. I saw you at the funeral, sorry about your uncle," Turner said. "Mabel

Lee can you grab this young fella a cup of coffee on me?"

"Morning," she said smiling at Terry.

"Good morning," Terry replied. "Thanks Sheriff," Terry said sitting next to him.

Mabel Lee was a fixture in the place. Pink flour-covered apron and bottle-blonde hair. She handed Terry a steaming cup of coffee and went back to work.

"Sheriff Turner, we had a break-in last night," Terry said. "I need to file a police report."

Terry described the events of the prior evening, leaving out some of the stranger details.

"Okay," Turner said. "I'll get one of my deputies out to your place this afternoon. Let them look around and see if we can get to the bottom of this situation. Mr. James, what made you all want to move out to that old place? Young couple like you might be more at home in South Ridge."

"Well," Terry answered, "my uncle left me the place, my wife and I thought we might try to turn the place into a B&B."

"Mr. James, there is a lot you need to learn about this area and you are going to find it mighty hard to get any folks to spend a night in the James lodge," Sheriff Turner said.

The sheriff excused himself and left the restaurant.

CHAPTER EIGHT

During the drive home Terry couldn't help but replay the conversation with the sheriff in his mind. Converting the lodge into a B&B seemed to be a solid idea. There were no homes or businesses of any kind outside of downtown Silverton. In fact, they had not seen an inn or hotel anywhere. Maybe the sheriff was being protective of the town? It would make for some good conversation when his cousin Brenda and friend Donald arrived for the weekend. Brenda and Terry spent a great deal of time together as children. She had been a sickly child, frequently hospitalized, and forced to endure a heart transplant at three months old. Most of her childhood was spent inside playing board games and watching TV. Later, when she was older, she claimed to see horrible things and was treated for psychosis. Brenda eventually overcame the troubles of her childhood and moved on with her life.

Donald had offered to help them get the place ready and was flying in on Saturday. He and Terry had worked together at Springside. Donald still taught American history at the school but Springside was rarely a topic of conversation between them. Terry glanced down at Abby's shopping list on the passenger seat.

"Dammit," he said as he swung the Jeep into a U-turn on the empty country road.

Abby finished unpacking and setting up their bedroom. Not knowing what type of furnishings they would find, they had left most of their belongings in a storage facility in Denver. Abby found the decorations in the lodge quite nice including the hand-carved log bed that dominated their bedroom.

Thankfully, the house was devoid of the dusty animal heads found in many country places. Abby noticed a thin strap made from a tree branch dangling behind the headboard. She reached and pulled out the strap which had a triangular carved medallion attached. The medallion was thin, but surprisingly heavy with iron inlays depicting two black birds.

She held the medallion up to the rear window and the light danced off the metal as it spun in the sunlight. From the window she saw the trail that led into the western woods and in the distance a modulating light. She placed the medallion into her pocket and the light in the woods disappeared. She retrieved the medallion and held it up to the window and the light was visible again.

CHAPTER NINE

Terry arrived home from the market and unloaded the groceries. Abby was setting the table when they heard a knock on the door.

"Joseph already?" she said.

Terry left the kitchen and walked through the great room to the front door. Opening the door he found Deputy Ima Rogers. She looked nervous and greeted Terry with a quick smile.

"Mr. James, I understand you had an incident last night?" Ima said as she flipped open a leather-bound notepad.

"Yes Deputy," Terry answered. "Please come in."

Ima stepped across the threshold as though stepping onto a ledge.

"Please have a seat," Terry said.

Ima sat in a chair close to the front door and began. "Mr. James, why don't you tell me what you saw last night?"

Terry sat down and recounted the evening's events for the deputy. Ima had her notebook in her lap but didn't write anything. Within a few minutes she glanced at her watch and said, "Thank you for your time. I will get my report submitted in the morning." She stood and walked to the front door.

"Good bye," she said.

"Deputy?" Terry called behind here. "Don't you want to look around?"

"No," she said quickly. "I've seen enough."

Ima climbed into her patrol truck and let out a deep breath. She was shaken and couldn't leave fast enough.

CHAPTER TEN

J oseph arrived for dinner at five-thirty sharp carrying wildflowers.

"Joseph, please come in," Abby said greeting him in the doorway. "Terry is out back grilling dinner. Please have a seat."

After serving Joseph a glass of tea, Abby sat in a chair across from him. She wore the medallion she'd found behind the bed, Joseph noticed immediately but didn't comment.

"Abby," Joseph began. "I think my comments earlier today may have confused you both, but I thought it was important for me to tell you about this area. The place where you came from is a world of black and white, night and day. The world here is very different and those differences must be understood and respected."

"Joseph," Abby said, "Terry and I are very sensitive to local traditions and customs."

Joseph spoke emphatically. "Abby this is not about customs. This is about life and death and the world between them both."

Abby sat blank faced trying to understand what he was saying.

"Picture the shore of a beach," Joseph said. "The sand is one part of the beach and the water another. In between is a third part that is constantly changing with the tides which is where the danger lies. The western wood is a place of change and during these times it can be deadly." Joseph looked up at a portrait of Ted hanging on the wall.

He took a sip of tea and continued. "Abby, I sense something in you, pulling you towards this place of change and it concerns me greatly."

"Joseph, how can I be pulled to something I don't even understand?"

"You do not need to understand it. You will find unusual things around here but you will find far worse in those woods after dark."

"Food's ready," Terry said walking into the room.

"Great." Joseph smiled. "I am appreciative of a home-cooked meal."

They sat enjoying the meal at a wooden table in the kitchen of the lodge. After the meal Terry and Joseph walked out back and sat on a stone veranda that overlooked the forest. It was dark and the only light was the glowing embers from the charcoal. The woods was a dark stain streaked across the green meadow. The river had stopped its southward flow and was perfectly still.

Joseph knew what would happen next, he and Ted had watched the river many times before. The water began moving again, this time flowing north.

"Terry, maybe we should move inside?" Joseph asked.

"Sure," Terry said.

The two men walked back into the lodge where Abby was finishing up the dinner dishes. Terry led Joseph down a long hallway to the pool room and grabbed a cue.

"Do you play Joseph?" he asked.

"No, but feel free," Joseph answered.

Terry racked the balls then walked behind the bar and found a bottle of wine.

"Looks like a Black Muscadine," Terry said looking at the label. "Would you like a glass, Joseph?"

"Sure. Thank you."

Terry poured two glasses of the bluish wine and handed one to Joseph.

"Cheers," Terry said.

"Cheers." Joseph raised his glass.

Terry cracked the cue ball and watched as the other balls settled around the table.

"Joseph," he said. "We found the room behind the bar. Someone was in the house and left it open."

Terry put down the pool cue and walked behind the bar. He pressed on the mirror door and it clicked open.

"We found it just like you see it now. Can you tell me what is going on around here?"

Joseph walked around to the open door and examined the mirror. "See this?" he asked. "The only marks on the glass are yours."

Terry examined the mirror and found a small smudge where he had pressed the dusty mirror.

"I guess you know what is behind this door, then?"

"Yes," said Joseph. "Ted showed this door to me many years ago. Sections of this lodge are very old. Your uncle thought this section of the house had been used by bootleggers years ago. He told me he had found other places like it over the years but I do not know them all. I do know that this house has a series of canals running underneath its structure. There was a settlement here over a hundred years ago. Your uncle believed the canals were dredged out by the settlers to protect themselves from evil. It's believed that water and other elements can provide a defense against the darkness."

Joseph gestured to the open mirror door. "In the cave below we found salts, herbs and symbols. People would float these items in baskets to protect themselves."

Joseph walked over and closed the mirror door.

"You will find other places like this throughout the house, usually behind mirror or glass. Your uncle believed that the reflective surfaces also created a barrier."

Joseph finished his wine then extended his hand and said, "Good night. It is getting late and I better be going."

The two men shook hands, and Terry walked Joseph into the great room.

"Abby?" Terry called out. She appeared from around the corner with a cake on a platter.

"You guys ready for some dessert?" she asked.

"Not for me," Joseph answered. "It's late and I must be going. Thank you both for dinner."

Joseph left through the front door and walked into the night air.

CHAPTER ELEVEN

B renda Collins looked at her reflection in the
mirror. She was pale with jet black hair and looked
tired. Last night was like many other nights. Two hours
sleep, tossing and turning, until she finally got up and
read. She had never slept a full night in her life. Since
childhood she had suffered from serious illness and
other issues, but it was the other issues that kept her
up at night. When she was younger she told the doctors
about the whispers and visions she experienced. By
the age of ten she realized telling the truth only made
things worse. She was fed one medication after another
and her parents feared she would be institutionalized.

"What would that cost?" she remembered her
mother saying in her shrill voice.

"She is not going anywhere," her father would answer. "Those damn doctors don't know their asses from a hole in the ground."

Brenda's father drank too much and swore too much, but she loved him all the same. He always had her best interests at heart and may have actually believed in the things she experienced. She thought of them as her distractions.

Brenda turned the page of the book while trying to filter out the whispers. She wouldn't allow herself a look at the corners of the room. Not because she was afraid, she had gotten over that a long time ago. In the living room of her rented house she knew she would see the repeated scene of a man and woman walking past. The misty gray-blue figures would walk by over and over again like a re-run that never went off the air.

She had experienced countless distractions in other places and they all repeated in the same way. The images and sounds varied and they appeared to be of different times. Sometimes they were adults, sometimes children or even animals. Occasionally, she thought they could sense her, but generally they wouldn't look at her or acknowledge her presence. She watched the cycles for hours, mesmerized.

Over time she learned not to stare at corners and hear whispers. At least she couldn't let anyone know she did. By the age of thirteen, she confessed to the doctors that she had lied about the visions, and made up the stories to get attention. Her mother was elated by the change; her father seemed strangely saddened. Either way, the meds and doctor visits decreased dramatically and Brenda moved on pretending to lead a normal life.

She closed the book and studied an unfinished painting standing on an easel. It needed more work but she would get back to it later. She had been commissioned to paint an historic lighthouse and still needed to have her neighbor Steven compare the photographs of the building to her painting. The painting only needed to capture what everyone else saw.

CHAPTER TWELVE

Joseph walked along the empty road finding the time had grown later than he'd realized. He quickened his pace while walking in the near dark. A branch snapped behind him, he stopped and stood very still, barely breathing. He continued walking and heard another snapping sound, the noise came from the woods. Joseph started to run.

He cut through the woods and moved swiftly down an overgrown path. Murmurs and knocks came from within the trees. He stopped and put a small bag of stones on a string around his neck, charms that would help protect him. He heard a crash in front of him, then behind him, and two more to his sides. He was trapped and boxed in by toppled trees. He snapped the string holding the bag and arranged the stones in a circle. Reaching into his pocket, he found a vial of dried herbs and the stub of a candle. He lit the candle and placed it on the ground, poured herbs between the rocks, then sat and waited.

Joseph knew if he stayed still within the stones he would be safe. He jumped to his feet when a burning tree fell in front of the circle but didn't leave the safety of the stones. The bark surrounding the burning tree cracked and inside something began scratching. The trunk of the tree broke open and a burning figure emerged. Joseph closed his eyes and did not look at the creature crawling towards him. He smelled burning flesh and knew it was near. The creature's face, just beyond the stone circle, oozed liquid from black eye holes. Joseph curled up on the ground, prepared to spend the night within the safety of the stones.

South of town, Ima sat on the steps of her apartment, smoked a cigarette, and stared at a half filled parking lot. She couldn't stop thinking about the way she felt up at the James lodge, panic and suffocation, as if the place would choke the life out of her. As a child, Ima spent much of her time playing in the woods. She was at home there. Why was it so different at the Lodge? The comfort she felt in nature was replaced by something festering unseen below the surface. Like most people in the area, she lived in South Ridge. With two hundred years of bad happenings, people gave Silverton a wide berth after dark.

Ima had been orphaned at a young age. Her father had been a full blood Cherokee and her mother a farmgirl from Minnesota, but she lost any connection with her father's heritage when her maternal grandmother became her guardian. Her birth name of Imala was shortened to Ima, and she was taught to hide part of who she was. Taught to focus on the modern world. She worked the night shift at the Sheriff's office and saw her share of domestic abuse, drunk driving and robberies. Some modern world.

At the lodge, Terry sat in a leather chair as Abby gathered up the empty cake plates and walked them into the kitchen. She came back into the room and sat on the couch with a pillow across her lap.

"Joseph had a lot to say tonight," Abby said. "You should open your mind to the possibilities of what Joseph is trying to tell us."

"I believe he means well," Terry said. "But I think we need to keep what he says in context. The man has lived in isolation for a long time which has sent his imagination spiraling out of control. Mix that with area legend and you get some pretty wild stuff."

"What about the intruder and the cave?" Abby said.

"Joseph mentioned there were other places like that cave in this house," he answered. "I think we have someone who is either a prankster or didn't realize the place was occupied. We need to locate any passages into this place and secure them, and when we do, these strange occurrences will end."

CHAPTER THIRTEEN

The morning sun shone through great room windows. Terry was up early and began a detailed search of the house starting with the great room. He examined the walls and mirrors tapping on them for any evidence of a passageway. He came upon an ornate mirror resting on the hallway floor. He ran his fingers over the elaborate scroll work on the frame and found a piece that moved. With a twist the mirror unlatched and swung open. Terry grabbed his flashlight then entered a doorway behind it.

He walked down into a cavern and found another water channel and a wooden canoe propped against the wall. Launching the canoe, he drifted towards an opening in the rock wall, slipped into a tunnel and floated deeper under the lodge. As the water in the channel began to churn and move faster, the paddle was wrenched from his hands and lost in the waters behind him. Rudderless, the canoe was battered against rough stone walls.

The boat slowed and drifted into another cavern, mist moved across the water, chilling him as it passed. On a muddy beach were large crows cawing, the sound deafening within the confines of the cave. He covered his ears as the birds launched themselves into the air, their feathers hung in mottled strands and bones protruded as they flapped skeletal wings.

The current pulled him into another tunnel where he saw the gray figure of a man, shoulder deep in water, hands turned towards the ceiling. The bow of the canoe passed through the man and Terry experienced the man's death by hanging. His head pounded with pain and then he vomited and fell back on the floor of the canoe. Passing through the creature took only a moment but Terry relived hours of torture. He was exhausted and shaking as the canoe drifted further.

An old woman stood in the water with her hands reaching for the ceiling of the tunnel. Searing pain rocked him as he passed through the woman and experienced her death by drowning. White foam sprayed from his mouth and he began convulsing. In the tunnel ahead was a group of white specters, arms outstretched waiting to share their pain. Terry dumped the canoe and plunged into the water. He groped for a hand hold and found tree roots poking through the ceiling of the cave. He pulled himself onto the side of the channel and saw light streaming in above him. A vertical column rose out of the tunnel, he climbed the walls, hanging onto roots and jagged rocks and then emerged in the middle of a dense forest where it was neither night nor day.

CHAPTER FOURTEEN

"Terry?" Abby called out.
She walked through the great room and into the hallway.

"Terry?" she called out again.

On the floor in the hallway were his tools and a pad of paper. She read the pad and found a list of furniture with check marks next to them. The mirror in the hallway was circled.

"Terry?"

She found the lever on the mirror and opened the door and was met with shadows and a damp smell.

"Terry," Abby called out. The sound of her voice reverberated into the unseen space.

Abby turned and walked towards the front door of the lodge, stopped and grabbed the keys to the Cherokee. She sped towards Joseph's cabin and turned at the stump in the road. Arriving at the cabin, she parked the truck, walked to the front porch and found Joseph's door open.

"Joseph?" Abby called out.

"Abby, is that you?" Joseph answered. "Please come in."

Abby walked in and found a tired looking Joseph sitting in a chair.

"Abby is something wrong?"

"Yes, I cannot find Terry."

She drove Joseph back to the lodge and led him directly to the mirror door.

"I'll get some flashlights," she said.

"That will not be necessary," Joseph said.

 He pulled a small red candle from his bag and lit it.

"Please allow me a few moments alone," he said.

Joseph walked into the dark opening and turned to face Abby.

"Please, close the door behind me and wait for my signal. If you hear anything else, do not open this door." He turned and walked through the doorway.

When Joseph was a small boy he developed the ability to track, not physical phenomena like broken twigs or foot prints but psychic phenomena, the trails of the living and the dead. In the candlelight he saw the faint vapor trail Terry had left behind. The trail was jerky and erratic and looked like dust in sunlight. Over the years, Joseph had learned to recognize the patterns of people he knew, the patterns of the living were deliberate and geometric, while those of the dead were soft and flowing. He followed Terry's trail until it flowed into the water.

"Terry?" Joseph called out.

Abby fidgeted in the hallway waiting for Joseph to return. Panic had begun to rise up in her when she heard a soft knock. She opened the mirror and Joseph emerged from the opening.

"He was here," he said. "Can he swim?"

"What?" she said.

"Can Terry swim?" he repeated.

"Yes, but why? What happened? Abby's voice grew high and panicked.

"We need to get to the woods."

CHAPTER FIFTEEN

J oseph led Abby to an outbuilding south of the lodge and swung open the doors. He pulled a tarp off a vehicle and threw it on the ground.

"Get in," he said pointing at an Argo eight-wheel vehicle.

Joseph cranked the engine until it fired up then revved the motor and drove out of the building to the woods. There was little time left before dark and the trees seemed to close in behind them as they raced into the forest.

Abby turned to Joseph and asked, "Should I call the sheriff?"

"Wouldn't do any good," he answered. "I doubt they would come here anyway."

The ATV tires clawed for traction on the rocky terrain when he slowed to navigate past a fallen tree. He knew the woods well enough having played there as a boy before the boundaries shifted. They reached a river crossing where the water rushed past rocks and roots jutted from the muddy river bank like tentacles.

"Hold on," he said as he dipped the nose of the amphibious vehicle into the river.

With a jerk the current grabbed the ATV and Joseph was able to maneuver the vehicle across the river.

"Abby, remember when I told you about the place of danger, the place of change?" Joseph asked.

She nodded.

"This is that place," Joseph said.

The trees cast shadows on the black earth of the forest floor and sounds were strangely muffled.

"Joseph, why is it so dangerous here?"

"In the early eighteen hundreds the town of Silverton became a hub for gold and silver mining. The town grew rapidly as did the greed for more land. The search for precious metals expanded and very quickly the townspeople demanded access to tribal lands which caused many border skirmishes. The leaders of Silverton struck a bargain with the tribal leaders, and agreed to rid them of a Raven Mocker that was terrorizing their people," Joseph said.

"A Raven Mocker?" Abby asked.

"Yes, a creature that devours the hearts of the living and the souls of the dead, a witch that hunts on tribal lands. Upon learning of the tribe's fears, the local townspeople agreed to intervene believing they would gain access to the tribe's lands for simply dispelling a myth."

Joseph conveyed the history to Abby. On June 7th, 1823, with the blessing of the tribe, a group of local men gathered up sacks of stones gathered from a sacred plot of tribal land. The men travelled by horseback deep into the mountains where the Raven Mocker was said to exist. After a half day's ride they arrived at a ramshackle cabin, an old woman sat on the porch and stared silently at the men. One by one the men dismounted their horses and unstrapped bags of stones, the sky overhead darkened as rain clouds began to form.

"She is just an old woman," Calvin Smith whispered to his partner Edmund.

The two men had been chosen to handle the mission. Calvin, Edmund and their men were popular in Silverton when unpopular things needed to happen.

"Who cares?" Edmund answered. "Her own kind wants her gone. It ain't no business of ours what she is."

With that said, Edmund gave the signal to start. The men, eleven in all, with sacks of stones at their feet, began throwing. The first nervous throws skipped off the rotted planks of the porch and one cracked through a dirty window. Calvin was the first to hit the women with a hard shot to the head, but she didn't flinch. She stayed silent, eyes unblinking as the stones rained down on her. The skies opened up and a drenching rain poured down which caused the men to throw faster and harder. The woman remained still with her hands gripping the arms of a timber chair.

After the last stone was thrown, they stood in the rain and assessed the damage. The bloody corpse of the woman remained seated with her fingernails stuck into the arms of the wooden chair. Her body was pried free, wrapped in a tarp and draped over the back of a mule. The men gathered up the stones as the rain pounded the muddy soil around them. The tribes had insisted that every stone was to be recovered and removed from Indian land. Lightning flashed across the black sky as they mounted their horses and rode off the mountain.

The men, exhausted and relieved to be down from the mountain, rode back into town.

"Where we headin Eddy?" Calvin asked Edmund.

"Them Indians didn't say nothing about what to do with the body and stones, other than to git it off their land. I know a little field with soft dirt where we can bury this hag," Edmund answered.

They rode into Silverton, eleven men, twelve horses and three mules made up their makeshift procession. Townspeople peered out from shop windows as they passed. They didn't expect a celebration having cleaned up the Indians' problem not Silverton's.

The men dismounted and unloaded shovels in a vacant field near the town's cemetery. Two of the men began digging and created a shallow grave. Edmund unrolled the tarp letting the body tumble into the grave. The blackened eyes of the corpse were open and staring.

The first shovel of dirt went over her eyes.

"Enough to give you the creeps," said one of the men as he piled dirt into the grave.

"Quit your talking and fill that hole," Edmund yelled at the man.

After the men finished filling the hole and tamping down the burial mound, Edmund instructed them to dump the sacks of stones onto the grave. The men untied the heavy burlap sacks and dumped the stones evenly across the grave. Edmund approached the grave, unbuttoned his trousers, and relieved himself.

"Remind me not to invite you to my funeral," one of the men yelled out which elicited nervous laughter from the men.

"All of the eleven men involved," Joseph said, "were dead within a month of the burial."

"How did they die?" Abby asked.

"Accidents and arguments mainly. I understand two men died in a gunfight over money, a few others were killed in a mine explosion. No one knows for sure what really happened to the rest of them. After that, the town fell on hard times and people headed south and gave up on the town altogether. According to tribal lore the Raven Mocker will only hunt on tribal lands, but these people scared easily and blamed the town's misfortune on the stoning. They believed that the worst was yet to come. In time, people did come back and the town began to prosper again but you will find that even today, few people stay after dark."

Joseph hit the brakes of the ATV and brought the vehicle to a stop, a burning tree lay across the path fifty yards ahead.

"Hold on," Joseph shouted as he spun the vehicle down an incline and into the depths of the forest. He stopped and hung a medallion, similar to the one Abby had found, from the roll bar of the machine.

"This will provide a small bit of protection," he said.

Abby held the swinging medallion as Joseph raced the ATV deeper into the forest.

CHAPTER SIXTEEN

After a few pained steps, Terry sat down and pulled off his boot. His ankle was swollen and flexing his foot caused a searing pain to radiate up his leg.

"Help," he yelled. His calls went unheard, muted by the dense woods.

He fashioned a makeshift walking stick and managed to get on his feet. Lost, with neither sun nor stars to guide him, he limped along for several hours until he found a cabin. Warm light emanated from the windows and smoke rose from a stone chimney. A young Indian woman sat on the porch and stared silently at Terry.

"Hello," he said hobbling towards the porch. "I'm sorry to trouble you. I've had an accident and need help."

The young woman stood and silently gestured towards the open door of the cabin.

"Thank you. My name is Terry James. I live nearby."

Terry limped past the woman and into the cabin. She gestured for him to sit at a small wooden table near a fireplace.

The young woman ladled a bowl of hot broth from a cast iron pot and placed it in front of him. He ate the warm broth, as the young woman gently picked sticks and leaves out of his hair. Suddenly his spoon turned cold and the broth putrefied in the bowl. He saw the hideous creature behind him in the oily reflection of the gruel.

He tried to get to his feet only to be slammed backwards in the wooden chair. The misshapen corpse of an old woman spiked its nails into his shirt and began to twist. He pulled a poker from the fire and plunged it into the creature's neck. The cabin filled with the smell of burning flesh. The creature grabbed his injured foot and twisted it backwards, the bone snapped and shattered through the skin. It then swung him through a glass window, where he landed face down in the dirt.

He fought for breath as his windpipe began to close. Struggling to breathe, he crawled across the ground until he reached the edge of a lake. The creature glided towards him with the poker dangling from its neck. Desperate, Terry plunged into the frigid water of the lake and was suddenly able to breathe again. He followed the shoreline out of site of the creature and found his canoe caught in a bramble of waterlogged tree roots. The canoe was half filled with water but he managed to right the canoe and escape into the safety of the lake.

CHAPTER SEVENTEEN

Joseph turned the ATV onto an abandoned dirt road, and drove to the shore of a lake.

"Abby, unfasten your seat belt," Joseph said. "This thing floats pretty well, but you don't want to be attached to it if something goes wrong. The water is deeper than you can imagine."

Abby complied, undoing her seat belt, and grabbed on to the roll bar for good measure. She nodded for Joseph to proceed and he drove into the water creating a wake that shimmered away from the vehicle.

"Abby you will see some disturbing things out here," Joseph said. "You must remain calm. I had hoped we would not need to cross these waters, but the woods will not allow us to pass."

"What if the water will not allow us to pass?" Abby asked.

"The water is different, neutral ground, a conduit for travel where powers are diluted."

Unseen things moved in the shadows as they drifted further into the lake. The vague outlines of submerged buildings hovered below them. Joseph turned the vehicle abruptly, avoiding a brick chimney jutting out of the water. A series of small islands came into view. On the first was a huddled mass of starving figures standing along the shoreline clutching tin pans. Elaborate tables filled with food lined the shore, but their sunken faces told Abby and Joseph the food was too late. Abby gasped and grabbed Joseph's arm.

"Easy Abby," he said. "We have a long way to go and it is best not to look."

The shadow of the next island fell over them as they passed and Abby stared into clenched hands.

"Abby," a mournful voice called out.

Her body stiffened.

"Ignore it," Joseph said.

"Abby," she heard again.

The voice coming from the island was sad and weak, but hauntingly familiar.

"Abby, help me," it said again.

Abby listened in shock to the voice of her sister Addie.

Ignoring Joseph's instructions, she looked at the island. Her sister stood in a white dress next to an overturned car. She recognized the dress; it was the one Addie was buried in.

"Stop," Abby yelled at Joseph. "That's my sister."

"Ignore it," Joseph replied staring straight ahead.

"We have to help her," she shrieked.

"She is beyond help."

Abby reached out and grabbed one of the control sticks causing the vehicle to pitch sideways. He pushed her back and steadied the craft.

"Abby," he yelled.

"Stop," she screamed.

Joseph brought the vehicle to a stop and it rolled from side to side in the water. The voice from the island continued to repeat its plea. Joseph reached into the back seat of the vehicle and pulled out a flashlight.

"Watch this," he said as he aimed the light at the figure on the island.

The figure moved in a repeating pattern, first with hands over its head, then hands outstretched, then arms wrapped around its torso.

"See the way the movements repeat?" Joseph asked.

Abby was sobbing with her knees pulled to her chest and didn't answer. Joseph continued sweeping the light across the figure whose pallid face was a black-and-white copy of Abby's. Each sweep of the light passed through the figure and the overturned vehicle near it.

"It's not real," he said softly. "It's not your sister."

Joseph navigated the vehicle away from the island and deeper into the lake.

CHAPTER EIGHTEEN

Donald dialed his phone and waited for an answer. "Hello."

"Brenda?" Donald asked.

"Yes, who is this please?"

"This is Donald Jensen, Terry's friend."

"Oh, Donald." Brenda sounded relieved. "I am so glad you called, I didn't have your number. Have you heard from Terry or Abby?"

"No," Donald answered. "I have been trying for days and haven't been able to reach them."

"I am driving up from Louisiana," she said. "I expect to get there late this evening."

"I am flying in tomorrow morning," Donald replied. "I should get up to Silverton by late afternoon. Should we contact someone else?"

"I don't know anyone else to contact other than the police," Brenda answered.

"I will call them right now," Donald said. "I'll let you know what I find out. Have a safe drive and don't worry, I am sure they are fine."

"Thanks Donald," Brenda said hanging up the phone.

"Sheriff's office," the voice on the phone line twanged.

"Hello my name is Donald Jensen. I am a friend of Terry and Abby James. They live up in the lodge outside of Silverton."

"I know who they are," Rita Haeckel said. "How can I help you?"

"I am afraid I have not been able to reach them for a several days. I am visiting tomorrow and cannot get in contact with them," Donald said. "I was wondering if you could send someone up to check on them."

"Surely," Rita answered. "If you want to try back in a couple of hours, we can let you know what we found out."

"Okay, thank you," Donald said.

"Bye," Rita chirped, gum clicking between her teeth.

Rita walked to the back of the office and found Ima pouring a cup of coffee.

"Deputy Rogers, we just received a call about the folks up at the James Lodge. Someone's looking for them and has not been able to reach them by phone."

"I will head up there right now," Ima responded.

Ima grabbed her jacket off the coat rack. On the wall next to it was a tarnished brass plate that read, safety is everyone's most important duty. Ima walked out the front door and surveyed the sky, rain was coming. She stepped off the curb and was startled by a crow flying overhead, its dark shadow barely visible in the gray sky.

Ima approached her truck and dropped her keys. She bent down to pick them up, and when she rose the crow was on the roof of her truck. She shooed the bird away and climbed into her truck.

CHAPTER NINETEEN

Terry heard the sounds of an engine and tried to sit up.

"Help, please help," Terry called out.

A horn sounded and he called out again, pounding his fist against the hull of the boat. He fell back, stared into the dull sky and lost consciousness.

Joseph and Abby heard Terry's cries. They were close to the shoreline and the compass in the vehicle spun wildly.

"Help." They heard the voice again, it was distant and weak.

Joseph did not need the voice or the compass. He was tracking his own way and had picked up the trail a few minutes earlier. The trail was getting stronger and he was confidant it was Terry's. Joseph adjusted course until they saw the shadow in the distance.

"Abby, I think we have found him," Joseph said.

"Thank goodness."

Joseph pulled alongside the canoe and grabbed the side of the craft. Terry lay in a pool of bloody water and the sight of his twisted leg made Joseph's stomach turn. Abby stood up and yelled to him.

"Abby!" Joseph said. "I need you to stay still and help hold the canoe."

"We need to get him out of there," she screamed.

"We cannot," Joseph answered. "If we try to move him we'll swamp us both, we need to tow him to one of the islands."

She complied as tears streamed down her face. Joseph tied the canoe to the back of the ATV and moved forward with the canoe in tow.

"Look," Abby said pointing towards a dark figure on the lakeshore. "Maybe it is someone who can help us."

"No," he said weakly. "That is not the way."

It was the Raven Mocker and he sensed its hunger.

He shuddered and said, "We need to go now."

Pulling the swamped canoe slowed them considerably and the best they could manage was a slow crawl. Joseph feared they would be trapped on the water after dark, but Terry needed to stabilized and brought into their vehicle.

An island came into view, and on the shore was a burning building with people jumping from its windows.

"We are not going there are we?" Abby asked.

"We must," Joseph answered. "I will land as far away as I can."

Joseph landed in a thicket fifty yards from the building and then drove onto the shore scraping the canoe over the rocky beach. He climbed out and arranged a circle of stones around them.

"This will provide protection, but we must be fast. There is too much pain in this place and we cannot remain for long," Joseph said.

He opened a trunk in the rear of the ATV and retrieved a first aid kit and a blanket. He placed the items on the front seat and said, "Help me lift him."

"Please be careful," Abby said through tear-filled eyes. "His leg…"

When they lifted him into the backseat, he came to and thrashed wildly, his injured leg a twisted mess of blood and bone.

"Abby, please hold him still," Joseph said.

Abby pressed down on Terry's shoulders. Joseph found a sedative in the first aid kit and injected him. He quieted which allowed Joseph to fashion a splint on Terry's damaged leg.

CHAPTER TWENTY

Ima arrived at the lodge shortly before sunset. She walked to the front door and rang the doorbell, but no one answered. A Jeep sat parked in the driveway, she felt the hood of the truck but it was as cold as the air around it. She walked around the back of the lodge to an outbuilding. Both doors were open and tire tracks led out of the building. She followed the tracks across a stone bridge and reached the edge of the forest. There, the tracks abruptly disappeared.

"Sheriff?" Ima called into the trucks radio.

"Hey Ima," Sheriff Turner answered.

"I'm up at the James Lodge. There's something strange going on here," she said.

"What's up, Ima?"

"We received a call that the folks up here couldn't be contacted. I've searched the grounds and there's something you should see."

"Any signs of foul play?" Sheriff Turner asked.

"No," Ima answered.

"Okay, then we need to pick it up in the a.m.," he said.

"But Sheriff," Ima started to say.

"In the a.m. You hear me deputy?"

"Yes sir," Ima answered. "Over and out."

She knew him well enough to predict his response. The sheriff's office patrol area ended way short of these parts after hours.

Ima opened the door of her truck and prepared to leave when she heard the sound of a car approaching. Moments later a silver Honda turned up the drive, the car's radio shattered the quiet. The car pulled to a stop and a slim, dark-haired woman emerged.

"Any sign of them?" Brenda called out.

"And you are? " Ima replied.

"My name is Brenda Collins. My friend Donald called your office."

"Sorry Miss Collins, we have not located them yet. Did you just arrive in Silverton?"

"Yes, I drove up from Louisiana."

"A loud radio helps keep me awake on a long trip as well," Ima said.

"Oh, yes. Yes it does," Brenda said.

Falling asleep was not the problem. The radio helped her mute the distractions, the sounds had been deafening since she drove into the mountains.

"I know you're probably tired from your drive, but if you have a few minutes, I would like to ask you some questions," Ima said.

"Certainly," said Brenda.

The two women walked to the front of the lodge. Ima grabbed the carved wooden handle of the door and pushed it open. She braced herself when she stepped inside. The claustrophobic feeling was there again, but she was able to keep it under control this time. When Brenda walked in, all of the distractions that filled her mind were stripped away.

CHAPTER TWENTY ONE

Abby and Joseph climbed into the ATV, the shoreline was a dim strip obscured by shadows. Bright orange flames engulfed the spectral building and burning people continued to jump. One of them jumped, hit the ground, and disappeared into the flames. The circle of fire surrounding the building opened and shot towards them. The jumper emerged from the flames and crawled towards the ATV. Joseph started the engine and backed the vehicle into the water. The creature was upon them, stopped only by the line of stones. Joseph piloted them away from the shore and into the safety of the lake. Steam rose from the creature's blackened flesh when it tried to follow them into the water.

The beam of the headlights disappeared into the fog hovering over the surface of the lake. Travelling in silence, the rumble of the engine was their only connection to the outside world.

Joseph finally spoke. "We needed those stones. I have nothing left to protect us."

"Can we make it back without them?" Abby asked. "Terry needs a doctor now."

"No. We would never make it back through those woods after dark."

He turned off the vehicle's engine and lights.

"I am afraid we will need to drift out here tonight," he said. "We cannot take our chances on land."

Joseph looked back at Terry.

"He is in shock, so we will need to keep him warm and calm. You should climb in the back with him and get some sleep."

Abby stepped over the seat and crawled under a blanket with Terry. He was cold and shivering, she wrapped her arms around his neck to warm him.

Joseph stared into the lake. It was quiet, yet he sensed a low hum like the sound of an electrical generator. When he was a boy, his people had used the lake and were not afraid. But things had changed, and the boundaries between the living and the dead had shifted. It began with a series of drownings. People swimming in calm waters were sucked under the surface and never seen again. The tribes in the area quickly abandoned these lands for safer places.

Joseph was one of the few who decided to stay and learned to co-exist here. Modern technology was unwelcome, clocks stopped, power went out, and batteries drained. Joseph became accustomed to these strange occurrences and, anyway, did not have much use for such conveniences. He passed his hand through the cold water and stirred away the mist. Dim lights appeared to glow below the surface. Legend had it that these waters connected to others areas, other worlds, but only the ones lost could really know.

Morning came and the lake was shrouded with a gray mist. Abby shook a sleeping Joseph. Terry was crying in terrible pain beside her.

"Joseph," she said. "Terry needs more medication."

"Of course," Joseph answered, still groggy.

He reached into his jacket pocket and handed a bottle of pain killers to Abby. She put two of the pills into Terry's mouth. His eyes were open slightly and his head rolled from side to side. Joseph looked towards the sky and decided on a direction then touched the medallion and started the motor.

"Joseph, do you know the way back?" Abby asked.

Joseph did know the way. They had intersected their original path.

"Yes, I know the way now," he answered.

CHAPTER TWENTY TWO

Brenda awoke on a leather couch in the great room where she had spent an hour answering Deputy Roger's questions the night before. The deputy had searched the house and found no evidence of foul play, Terry and Abby had simply vanished. She had promised to return in the morning with additional help, and gave Brenda her cell number in case Terry and Abby showed up during the night.

Brenda walked into the kitchen and noticed movement through the back windows. Abby and a man were driving towards the lodge. She ran into the great room and pulled her cell phone from her purse.

"Hello," she heard on the other end. "This is Ima Rogers."

"Deputy Rogers this is Brenda. Abby is back."

"Is she okay?" Ima asked.

"I don't know yet. I can see her coming from the woods," Brenda answered.

"I'll be there in ten minutes," Ima said and hung up.

Brenda saw them headed towards the drive at a high rate of speed. She ran out the front door to meet them, and found them parked next to Terry's truck. Abby and the man lifted something into the back of the Jeep. Brenda called out as she crossed the gravel drive.

"Abby, what happened?" Brenda asked.

Abby turned and looked at Brenda. It took a moment for Abby to comprehend that she was actually there.

Finally Abby choked out, "Terry is hurt."

Brenda ran up to the back hatch of the truck, Terry was wrapped in a blood soaked blanket and looked pale. Abby and the man appeared dazed and exhausted.

"Where are the keys? I can drive," Brenda said.

"On the table by the front door," Abby's answered in a weak voice.

Brenda dashed into the lodge and came back with the keys. They climbed into the truck and Brenda accelerated down the driveway.

"Which way?" Brenda asked.

"I will show you the way," Joseph answered, pointing to the south.

When they reached the emergency entrance for the South Ridge Medical Center, Brenda and Joseph rushed in to find help. Within moments, two orderlies and a nurse burst through the door wheeling a gurney. They removed the blanket to assess the extent of Terry's injuries. The team stabilized his damaged leg and rushed him directly into surgery.

Joseph, Brenda and Abby sat in the waiting room.

"Abby, what happened?" Brenda asked.

All Abby could say was, "It was horrible. It was horrible."

She started crying and Brenda leaned in to comfort her.

"Maybe we can discuss the details later?" Joseph asked. "The important thing is Terry is safe now."

"Okay," Brenda said.

A phone rang and they all jumped, Brenda fumbled in her pocket and answered it.

"Hello," she said into the phone. "Yes Deputy Rogers I found them. Terry is injured. We took him to South Ridge Medical Center. Okay, we will see you when you get here."

Twenty minutes later Ima Rogers hurried through the doors of the waiting room. She walked over to greet them and noticed that Joseph Wood was with them. He was known as a hermit and she had never actually spoken to him.

"Mrs. James, could I have a word with you?" Ima asked.

"Deputy Rogers, may I?" Joseph gestured to an examination room.

Ima followed Joseph into the room and he closed the door behind them.

"She is in shock, deputy," Joseph said glancing through the window at Abby.

Ima gathered her thoughts then pulled out a pad of paper and a pen and said, "Ok, why don't you tell me what happened?"

Joseph relayed the story in its entirety. Ima, who had been writing the details, closed her pad and threw it on the table.

"You are telling me a witch attacked Mr. James?" Ima said exasperated.

"We cannot be sure until Terry wakes, but yes, I believe that is what happened," Joseph answered.

Ima left the room without saying a word, and then walked back over to Abby.

"Mrs. James, I am happy you are all safe. I'll stop back this evening to check on you." She put on her deputy's hat and left.

Brenda walked into the hallway. Machines hummed softly in the quiet hospital. The sounds were comforting to her because they masked the whispers in the hallway. She looked at her watch, picked up her cell phone and dialed.

"Hello," Donald answered.

"Donald it's me, Brenda."

"Brenda, have you heard anything?" Donald asked.

"Yes, I found them. We are at the hospital."

"What happened?"

"We don't know yet," Brenda answered. "When will you be here?"

"In a few hours, I just picked up my rental car."

Dr. Avery Jacobs came in to the waiting room and approached Abby.

"Mrs. James, your husband is doing well," Dr. Jacobs said. "We operated on his leg. He sustained both a broken fibula and tibia. We inserted a titanium rod in his leg to stabilize the bones. We also treated him for severe hypothermia and dehydration. He has a long recovery ahead of him, but all in all he is doing remarkably well."

"Thank you, doctor," Abby said with tears running down her face.

"He is heavily sedated. I recommend you go home and get some rest and come see him this evening," Dr. Jacobs said.

"That sounds like good advice," Brenda said. "Come on, Abby." Brenda gently took her hand.

"Excuse me for a moment," Joseph said.

He walked into a hallway, located Terry's room and slipped inside. He arranged a mix of herbs into a protective circle under the bed and placed the medallion from the ATV in the middle. Closing the door behind him, he returned to the waiting room and helped Brenda get Abby to the parking lot and into the truck.

CHAPTER TWENTY THREE

When they approached the turn off to the lodge, Joseph said, "Brenda can you keep driving? I plan to stay at the lodge tonight but need to pick up a few things."

"Sure," Brenda replied. "Just tell me when to turn."

Brenda followed Joseph's instructions, turned onto the dirt road and pulled to a stop in front of his cabin.

"I will only be a few minutes," Joseph said.

He got out and walked into the unlocked front door of the cabin. Abby was asleep in the back seat. Brenda opened her window and let cool air wash over her. The whispers were there but quieter during the daytime. After a few minutes, Joseph came back with his arms loaded.

"Brenda, could you open the hatch?" Joseph asked.

She got out and did so. He organized clothing, a polished wooden box and a leather satchel in the back of the truck.

She drove them back to the lodge and found Donald's burgundy rental car parked in the driveway. Joseph gathered his items from the back and walked towards the lodge. Brenda woke Abby and helped her out of the back seat.

Entering the lodge, Joseph said, "I will start a fire and find something for us to eat. Brenda, can you get Abby up to bed by yourself?"

"Sure," Brenda answered.

There was no sign of Donald, other than a plaid suitcase sitting on the floor of the foyer. Brenda helped Abby up the carved staircase and down the hall to her bedroom. The carvings that covered the hallway walls were less noticeable during the daytime, but Brenda recognized many of them. They were protective symbols.

Abby changed clothes and slid into bed.

"Try to get some sleep Abby," Brenda said.

Brenda examined the medallion by Abby's bedside. The dense metal was heavy and etched with an intricate design. She put the medallion down and walked into the hallway, closing the door behind her. She ran her fingers across the markings on the wall reveling in the calmness of the place, then walked downstairs and into the kitchen where Joseph was stirring a pot on a cast iron stove.

"Soup okay?" he asked.

"Sounds great," Brenda answered.

Joseph looked at Brenda while they ate. She was young but also old, surrounded by the trail of the living mixed with the trail of the dead. Brenda was a seer and maybe more. She appeared frail but had been strengthened by her experiences, having endured much for someone so young.

"You are probably wondering what happened out there?" Joseph said gesturing to the back windows of the lodge.

"Yes, and about this place," Brenda answered.

Joseph explained the events in detail, needing Brenda to understand what they had encountered. He described the horrific things they had witnessed and explained the nature of the area. She had visited places where images and sounds leaked through, but this was something much larger and more dangerous.

"What about this house? Why is it so ... quiet?" Brenda asked.

"Because it is a fortress," Joseph answered. "Built to shield its inhabitants from the outside. Your uncle was a collector and became increasingly fascinated by protective objects. This place is full of them. You can see for yourself." Joseph gestured around the room.

Brenda never really knew her uncle Ted.

"What happened to him?" she asked.

"The coroner ruled it a heart attack but didn't order an autopsy. If he had, he would have discovered that Ted's heart was missing," Joseph answered.

"What?" Brenda exclaimed.

"The Raven Mocker. It took Ted's heart and consumed it."

Brenda sat silently absorbing what Joseph had described to her.

"Hello?"

Brenda rose and found Donald standing in the front doorway. He closed the door behind him and walked into the great room.

"It's been a long time," he said with a smile.

"Yes, it has. I'm really glad you're here," she answered. "Come in and sit. There is a lot to catch you up on."

CHAPTER TWENTY FOUR

Abby woke in the dark room. She dressed and walked down the hallway that overlooked the sprawling great room and found Brenda unpacking in a small guest room.

"Hello," Abby said slowly.

"Oh, Abby. Are you feeling better?" Brenda asked walking over to hug her.

"Yes, I needed to sleep," she answered.

She still looked tired, her hair was disheveled and dark circles lined her eyes.

"Why don't you come downstairs? I'll fix you something to eat," Brenda asked.

"No. I need to see Terry," Abby answered.

"Okay, I'll drive you over to the hospital."

Brenda placed the clothes she was folding on the bed and walked Abby downstairs. Joseph slept on the couch with a book on his chest.

"Joseph?" Brenda said gently shaking his shoulder.

Joseph awoke with a start and the book fell on the floor. Out of it fell numerous hand-drawn symbols similar to the wall carvings throughout the lodge. Brenda kneeled to pick up the pages and handed them back to Joseph.

"Sorry Joseph. I didn't mean to startle you. I'm taking Abby to the hospital to see Terry. Do you want to go along?" she asked.

"Yes of course. Just give me a moment to gather my things."

"Okay, let me find Donald to see if he would like to join us," Brenda said.

The four of them got into Brenda's car and drove to the hospital. She turned the radio to an oldies station to quiet the sounds only she could hear. They arrived in the near empty parking lot a few minutes before visiting hours ended, the floors had just been cleaned and the smell of bleach hung in the air. After signing in, a nurse showed them to Terry's room.

"He's still out, but I'm sure he will appreciate all the visitors," the nurse said with a smile. "A deputy arrived a few minutes ago. She is in with him now."

Ima sat in a chair beside Terry's bed and stood as they entered.

"Good evening," she said and nodded.

Abby took Terry's hand, a monitor beeped in rhythm with his heartbeat as he lay sedated. A nurse entered the room and bumped into a tray, spilling a pitcher of water. The water ran across the floor and under the bed.

"Oh, my," she said. "Let me get someone to clean that up. I am so sorry."

Joseph checked the protective circle under Terry's bed and found the water had washed it away. A tree crashed through the window as he reached for his bag. Shattered glass flew across the room knocking Abby to the floor. She scrambled across the room trying to get to her feet. The tree hung across Terry's bed and was wedged against the inside of the door. Hospital staff pounded outside trying to enter the room.

Abby made it across the floor with her hands punctured by broken glass. Mist spiraled up the trunk of the tree and along its branches, then twirled and formed into a blackened corpse with a skeletal frame. Wet clumps of gray hair hung across its face and jagged teeth lined black lips.

Joseph stepped forward and raised the medallion over his head. "Raven Mocker, cease!" He yelled.

The creature ignored Joseph's command, dropped off the branch and landed on Terry. Joseph struggled to fight through the tangled mass of branches as the creature ripped open Terry's gown. With a quick thrust, its claw punctured Terry's chest and then emerged with his glistening heart. The electronic monitor's alarm sounded as his heartbeat was lost.

Abby's screams filled the air and gunshots rang out. Ima's first shot hit a branch but the next three hit their mark, each with a sickening wet thud. Unaffected, the creature devoured Terry's heart and licked away the blood. It ran a claw across his chest and sealed the jagged wound. The beast then changed into a black bird, flew out the broken window and disappeared into the night sky.

They stood stunned as hospital staff continued to pound on the door. Abby's screams turned into uncontrollable sobbing and Ima stood wild-eyed clutching her gun. Joseph and Donald worked to pry open the door.

"Move back everyone," Joseph urged.

He pulled the door partly open, giving them enough space to escape the room. Within a matter of minutes, doctors and nurses flooded the room unaware that Terry was beyond help.

Abby was treated and released from the hospital and Brenda and Donald drove her home. Ima followed behind with Joseph in her patrol vehicle. They arrived back at the lodge after dark then sat in the great room staring numbly at the fireplace.

CHAPTER TWENTY FIVE

Ima paced around the great room, she would have to explain to the sheriff why she discharged her weapon in a hospital room. She was stressed and the no bullshit inner cop came out.

"We need to get our heads together on this thing," she said. "I need a statement from each of you."

Joseph protested initially but relented.

"Joseph, I am sorry," Ima said. "The sooner I get everyone's description of the incident, the more accurate the information."

Ima sat at the kitchen table and collected all of the statements, except Abby's. She was sedated and incoherent and would have to come later. Ima picked up the statements and re-read them. The accounts were all identical and matched her recollection perfectly but if they were submitted, she would be pulled for a psych exam.

Joseph walked into the kitchen and said, "Deputy, what do you plan to report?"

Ima threw down the statements and said, "Not these."

"Then we need to craft something you can submit," Joseph said. "And we need a plan." He continued, "But it is late and we should get some rest. I would strongly recommend you remain in this house tonight."

"Okay," Ima agreed.

They walked back into the great room where the fire gave the room a warm amber glow. Donald and Brenda sat on a leather couch across from a sleeping Abby.

Joseph stood to the side of the mantelpiece and spoke. "We should be safe if we stay in this house, but I recommend you do not go outside for any reason until the morning time."

"How do we know that thing won't smash in another window?" Until then, Donald had not said a word since they left the hospital.

"It cannot, this house has been insulated against outside forces. We are safe as long as we remain inside," Joseph answered.

"Why did it kill Terry?" Brenda asked.

"I am not completely sure," Joseph answered. "I believe he may have crossed paths with the creature in the western woods but I don't know how it left the confines of the forest, it draws power from the energy there."

Joseph stoked the flames, sat down in a leather chair and recounted the story of the stoning he had told Abby a few days earlier.

"There must be a historical record of those times," Donald said. "I will go into town in the morning to see what I can find."

"I have something that may be of assistance to you," Joseph said. "Follow me."

Joseph walked Donald down a hallway to a flight of stairs made of polished stone. They continued past a half dozen empty rooms and came to the end of the hallway, where sitting against the wall was a large framed mirror. The frame was carved and stained a dark mahogany and the glass was painted black. Joseph grabbed the mirror and slid it to the side and behind it was a room. He reached in and flipped on the lights revealing stacks of books covering the floor. Beyond the books was a cherry desk presiding over a cluttered library.

"What is all of this?" Donald asked.

"This is the history of Silverton. It was to be thrown away," Joseph said. "The town was ashamed of the things that happened here and planned to destroy the truth. When Ted found out, he asked me to help him procure the documents. We broke into the basement of the courthouse and took them all, then started a fire to cover up the theft. The brick building was completely gutted, but Ted sent a donation to pay for the repairs."

"I bet that caused quite a stir in town," Donald said. "Did they ever suspect anything?"

"No," Joseph answered. "There were many theories, but none of them ever pointed to us. Ted's donation made sure of that. He was a clever man."

Donald walked along the bookcases with his fingertips gliding over the bindings.

"These appear to be organized by date and time," Donald said. "But I need to go through them," he gesturing at the stacks of books on the floor. "This could take a while. I better get started right away."

"I will leave you then," Joseph replied.

Joseph left the room and closed the mirror door behind him. Donald settled behind the desk and wiped away the dust. He noticed chalk markings on the back of the door which laid out the system of organization in the room. One stack labeled Smith stood alone in the middle of the room and contained a variety of documents including ledgers, historical records, plot maps, and books. He gathered these up and organized them across the desk, then found a pen and pad of paper and began his research.

Joseph walked into the great room and found the last embers of the fire dying away. Abby and Brenda had both gone to bed and Ima was asleep on a couch tucked in an alcove under the stairs. Ima's service revolver was next to her on a plank wood coffee table. Joseph switched off the lights and walked upstairs to a corner room at the end of the hall.

CHAPTER TWENTY SIX

The morning sunlight poured into the great room and Ima woke with a start. She looked at her watch and saw it had stopped. Her uncle had given her the watch when she was a child. He had warned her it had brought him bad luck but for Ima, gifts and luck were both hard to come by. She wound the watch and it began to tick loudly. Climbing off the couch, she walked into the kitchen and found Donald pouring coffee, dressed in the same clothes as the night before.

"Find anything?" Ima asked while looking in the cupboard for a cup.

"Cups are over there," Donald said quickly. "Yes, I did find quite a bit, actually. Piecing it together is another story," he said. "Once everyone is up, I would like to discuss what I found."

"Joseph is out back," Ima said. "I can see him along the river."

Donald looked out and saw Joseph sitting on a stone bench.

"Great," Donald said. "I need to speak with him."

He stepped into the crisp morning air, sunlight streamed through oak trees and the field behind the lodge teemed with birds. He walked down from the stone veranda and followed a worn path in the grass to the spot where Joseph sat.

"Joseph," he called out.

Joseph turned and waved him over.

"Good, you are up. There are some things I must show you," Joseph said.

"Never actually slept," Donald replied. "There was a lot to go over."

Joseph stood, put his hand on Donald's shoulder and pointed towards the river.

"Look at the two sides of the water," he said.

The river had a blue aura and the current appeared to run in two directions.

"Wow," Donald said. "That's an interesting illusion."

It's no illusion," Joseph answered. "Follow me."

Joseph grabbed a handful of grass and walked out to the middle of the bridge where they both looked down at the river. He sprinkled grass on one side, which headed south then sprinkled grass on the other and that headed north.

"That's impossible," Donald said.

"Yes it is," Joseph answered. "Yet it just happened."

The two men walked over the bridge to the edge of the forest where Donald became suddenly confused as feelings of panic took hold of him. Joseph put a reassuring hand on his arm.

"Easy, Donald," he said. "Let's go back."

They stepped back onto the bridge and Donald experienced a rush of senses. The sounds of the birds, and the water and the wind returned to him.

"What just happened?"

"That was the power of the other side. It can take some getting used to."

Joseph led him back to the lodge where Ima and Brenda were consoling Abby. She sat in a daze with an untouched cup of tea in front of her.

"It's time we talked," Joseph announced to the group. "I think we all realize that the deputy cannot report what actually happened last night. We need to get our stories together so we are on the same page."

Joseph nodded to Ima, who handed out revised statements with any reference to the Raven Mocker omitted.

"But that isn't true," Abby shrieked. "The police will not help us if we don't tell them what happened."

Brenda moved in to calm her.

"Abby, they will not believe the truth," Brenda said.

Abby swept the statement onto the floor.

"I will not sign this," she screamed. "Terry is dead and that thing killed him."

Abby broke down into a fit of sobbing. Brenda helped her up and walked her towards the stairs.

"I will get her back up in bed," she said.

Abby's cries echoed through the great room.

"We'll be fine without her statement. I will tell the Sheriff she was too upset to give an interview," Ima said.

"What about you," Donald asked Ima.

"I'll be looking at a suspension for accidentally discharging my weapon, could be a couple of weeks," Ima answered.

"Ima, once you file your report you should come back here," Joseph said. "We all need to stay together in a safe place and this is the only safe place right now."

"Agreed," said Ima. She put on her jacket and took out her keys. "I'll be back before dark."

Joseph walked her out, bolted the door and then walked back to the kitchen. Brenda returned and sat at the kitchen table in front of a cold cup of coffee.

"Last night I saw something unusual. My visions are repeating loops playing scenes over and over again," Brenda said.

Donald and Joseph listened intently.

"I saw a man ... he looked like a settler, dressed in boots and clothing from years past and he was searching for something. I watched him over and over again," Ima finished.

"What was he looking for? Donald asked.

"I don't know," Brenda answered. "But it was very important to him."

"Can you describe the man, Brenda?" Joseph asked.

"Yes, he was tall and lanky, with pale, pock-marked skin and black hair. He wore a worn frock coat."

Donald stood up from the table and left without saying a word, then came back a few minutes later with a framed portrait covered in dust.

He held it up so Brenda could see it and said, "Is this the man?"

She hesitated. "Yes ... but who is it?"

"This is Calvin Smith," he answered. "A distant relation of yours."

"May I?" she asked.

Donald handed her the painting. She stared closely at the image before saying anything.

"This is definitely the man from the vision," she said. "The man who was searching for something lost."

CHAPTER TWENTY SEVEN

A grim-faced Ima returned late in the afternoon carrying a suitcase and wearing street clothes. Donald, Brenda and Joseph were reading through archives at the kitchen table while Abby stared vacantly at a fire in the great room.

"They bought it," Ima announced. "And I bought a two-week suspension."

They sat in silence for a few moments.

Joseph finally spoke. "Ima, we have something we need your help with.

"Brenda had a vision and we need every detail documented," Donald added. "We think it may help us with a plan."

"You got it," Ima said. "At least I can still act like a cop."

She sat across from Brenda on the couch in the great room alcove.

"Okay," Ima started. "Let's take it from the top."

Brenda recounted her vision while Ima took notes.

"How many times did this repeat?" Ima asked.

"A dozen times, maybe more. It's hard to say for sure. When it happens, I lose track of time and my surroundings."

"How did it end?" Ima asked.

"I fell asleep. I always fall asleep," Brenda answered. "When I was a child, the doctors believed I was suffering from bad dreams. But my visions were real, so I began researching them and found out that what I saw really happened in the past."

"Like a movie reel," Ima said.

"Yes," Brenda agreed.

Ima and Brenda joined Joseph and Donald in the kitchen as the light in the windows faded. They sat down at the table and Ima went through the details.

"Here is what we have so far," she said. "According to Brenda's description and Donald's research, it appears that the man in the vision is Calvin Smith. We know that Mr. Smith is related to Brenda, as well as Terry James and Ted James. Both deceased," Ima paused. "Based on Donald's research into the Silverton archives, we know that Calvin James was paid the sum of five hundred dollars to organize a group of vigilantes and was involved in the stoning death of an unnamed woman in 1823."

"But he never got to spend it," Donald jumped in. "His partner, Edmund, shot him in the back during an argument a week later. Edmund was hung soon after. In fact every man involved in the stoning was dead within the month. Many from unknown causes, they simply dropped dead."

"Like Terry," Brenda interjected. "And Ted."

"Joseph, what can you tell us about Ted's death? Ima asked.

"Heart attack is what the police report indicated," Joseph answered. "But that's not what happened. Towards the end of his life, Ted spent all of his time in the woods and sometimes even slept out there. He refused to let me accompany him."

"Did he say why?" Ima asked.

Joseph shook his head and said, "No, Ted never explained anything."

Joseph smiled as he remembered his friend.

"One night he left and didn't return. The next morning I found his body across the stone bridge. It looked like he had been running from something."

Joseph brushed a hand through his long grey hair and closed his eyes for a moment.

"I will never forget the look on his face," Joseph finished.

"Why didn't you warn us"? Abby's shriek filled the air. No one had noticed her in the door way.

"Abby, I tried to explain," Joseph started.

"You explained nothing," she screamed.

Brenda jumped up to calm her but Abby pushed her into the wall.

"Abby," Donald said jumping to his feet to restrain her.

Ima bent beside Brenda and examined the back of her head. She had a small gash on the back of her scalp.

"I'm okay," Brenda said.

She stood up and put her arm around Abby.

"Help me get her upstairs and back into bed," Brenda said looking at Donald.

"Sure," Donald said.

Brenda helped Abby into bed and gave her a glass of water to wash down a sedative. Donald stood nearby and studied the hieroglyphics like engravings on the walls. The symbols, a mix of animal and elemental shapes, appeared to be carved over varying time periods with the darkest and oldest lower on the wall.

"She's asleep," Brenda said closing the bedroom door behind them.

"Good. Poor thing must be out of her mind with grief," Donald said.

Brenda and Donald walked downstairs and into the kitchen.

"Is Abby okay?" Joseph asked.

"Yes," Brenda answered. "We gave her something to help her sleep."

"How about you, Brenda?" Ima asked. "How's your head?"

"I'm fine. Nothing an aspirin and a good night's sleep won't fix," Brenda answered.

"Brenda, with your permission, let's continue to review what we know," Joseph said.

"Yes, please Joseph," Brenda said.

"That thing that killed Terry may be after us," Ima started.

"The Raven Mocker," Joseph corrected, "is after us all. It feeds on revenge and hatred and my guess is Calvin Smith and the men who attacked the beast were tricked into antagonizing it. The tribe would never have allowed their sacred lands to be desecrated, even if it meant killing this witch. The tribe knew the townspeople could never set foot on the land once the Raven Mocker was disturbed."

"But what about the tribe?" Donald asked. "Weren't they afraid?"

"Yes, but they were willing to sacrifice the use of their lands in order to protect them from outsiders," Joseph answered. "The plan worked. Not a single tree has been felled since that day and the power of this place has grown in magnitudes ever since."

"How can we kill this thing?" Ima asked. "I shot it at least twice and it didn't even flinch."

Joseph stood and looked out the kitchen window, it had grown dark and raindrops made a pinging sound as they hit the metal roof.

"It can't be killed," he answered without turning around. "It will not stop until its thirst for revenge and hunger for hearts has been satisfied."

He sat at the table and cupped his hands together in front of him. "However, it can be trapped."

He turned to Donald and said, "I will need your help with something later tonight. But now, I need you to find out every detail about the stoning and to figure out what Calvin Smith was searching for."

"Sure," Donald replied.

Donald rose and left for the study. "Goodnight, it's time for me to get some rest," Joseph said.

Ima stood and stretched her arms over her head. "I'm going to go get some sleep as well."

"Goodnight," Brenda said. "Doubt I will be able to sleep much tonight. I think I'll go down and help Donald."

"Goodnight," Ima replied and padded over to the alcove couch.

After a few hours of restless sleep, Joseph woke. A trunk sat in the corner of his room, an ornate dome top with brass hinges and polished wood slats. He slid it to the side and revealed an opening in the floor, then climbed down a circular staircase to an unfinished hallway which ran unseen behind the walls of the lodge. He navigated the unlit hallway and slipped through a hidden panel into the closet of the study. Donald was slumped over the desk and Brenda was wrapped in a quilt asleep on a brown leather couch. He walked over to Donald and shook his shoulder.

Donald awoke with a start. Joseph put his hand to his mouth and whispered, "Quiet."

He led Donald to the closet, through the panel and into the hidden hallway.

"What is this place?" Donald asked.

"It is an escape way built by bootleggers," Joseph answered. The corridor was lined with rough timbers and mortar. Joseph continued, "It leads to various points within the lodge and the surrounding grounds."

Donald followed behind Joseph until they reached an exterior door. Cold air greeted them when they stepped into the woods. The outer door was camouflaged to blend in with the trees, Donald watched as it swung closed and disappeared into the foliage. He followed Joseph to the Jeep parked at the end of the drive.

The hatch was open with a tarp and shovels packed in the back.

"Sorry for the secrecy," Joseph said. "I didn't want to wake the others. Ima is in enough trouble already and I don't want to involve her in this."

"In what," Donald asked. "What exactly are we doing?"

"We are going to retrieve the remains of the Raven Mocker," Joseph answered.

CHAPTER TWENTY EIGHT

A breeze swayed the pines along the winding ribbon of the road and the first shimmers of orange light appeared in the eastern sky.

"Where are we going?" Donald asked.

"We are going into Silverton," he answered. The creature is weakest before sunrise so we need to move quickly."

The road, which had no guard rails, ran only feet from the edge of a deep ravine. Donald grasped for a handhold when Joseph swerved to avoid a black bird in the road.

"Shit what was that?" Donald asked.

"A warning," he answered. "We need to hurry."

They reached the edge of town as the yellow glow of the sun appeared above the horizon. Founded in the 1800s, Silverton's town square was a collection of buildings centered on a brick courthouse. Joseph pulled the Jeep into a field near the graveyard and caught the stone pile in the beam of the headlights.

"This is it," he said.

Joseph got out of the truck, retrieved the shovels and tarp and said, "We must be fast. People do not come back into town until daybreak, but sometimes the sheriff arrives earlier."

The two men shoveled the stones onto the tarp, and then dug into the oily black earth digging up clumps of dirt and bone. The stench sickened Donald. He stumbled away from the pile and vomited onto the ground. Composing himself, he straightened up and wiped his mouth with a handkerchief.

"Jesus," he said. "That smells horrible."

Joseph nodded and then began sprinkling herbs around the putrid mix. When completed, he folded the corners of the tarp and then tied them together with a strand of rope.

"Give me a hand," Joseph said.

The two men grappled with the load and swung it into the back of the truck. The soil surrounding the empty grave was scorched black with claw marks raking the inside of the hole. They drove back to the lodge with the windows open, preferring the cold air to the stench of their cargo.

Ima and Brenda were waiting in the driveway when they returned.

"Where were you?" Ima asked when the two men got out of the car.

"We had something important to do," Joseph answered.

"Where's Abby?" Brenda asked.

"Not with us," Donald said.

"She's not in her room," Brenda said. "We thought she was with you."

Joseph walked off behind the lodge without saying a word. Donald was explaining what they had done when he returned in the ATV.

"Abby has gone into the woods," he said.

"How do you know?" Ima asked.

"I just know."

"Donald help me here," Joseph said.

The two men wrestled the tarp into the back seat of the ATV. Donald ran ahead to the lodge and swung open the front doors allowing Joseph to drive through the great room and down the hallway to the mirror. Joseph opened the mirror and drove down to the floor of the cave. Donald called out from the hallway above.

"Joseph?"

"Yes Donald, down here."

Donald followed the lights of the ATV through the darkness and down the stone steps. "What is this place?" he asked.

"This lodge is a fortress and this is part of its defenses. Unlike most castles, this one was designed to keep out the spirit world rather than invaders and cannon fire."

Donald ran his hand across the cool smooth walls of the cave.

"Solid granite," Joseph said. "The entire structure sits on granite bedrock. There are elements embedded within the stone that emit a natural radiation which prevents energy from penetrating."

"What about the water?" Donald asked.

"These channels were carved into the bedrock to direct water flow from the river. This essence of life is an attractant to the spirit world and also a barrier against dark things which will resist crossing it. Help me with this," Joseph said grabbing a corner of the tarp.

The two men heaved the tarp onto the stone floor.

"Now we must find Abby before nightfall," Joseph said. "Get in," he said gesturing to the ATV.

Joseph started the engine which created a deafening roar in the cave. He maneuvered the vehicle up the stone steps and out the front doors of the lodge where Brenda and Ima came out to meet them.

"What about Abby?" Brenda asked.

"Donald and I will go find her," Joseph answered.

"I'm going too," Ima said.

"Me too," Brenda added moving towards the ATV.

"You need to stay Brenda, in case Abby shows up here," Joseph said.

"But I can help find her. You know that Joseph."

Joseph nodded in agreement and grabbed the controls of the ATV. Donald climbed in beside him with Brenda and Ima in the back. Ima pulled her gun from its holster, chambered a bullet and held the weapon with two hands.

"That will not help here," Joseph said.

"Let's see about that," insisted Ima.

CHAPTER TWENTY NINE

They sped across the field and onto the bridge, the knobby tires reverberated until they crossed over and the world went quiet.

Brenda clasped her hands over her ears and began to scream, "No!"

Joseph hit the brakes and the vehicle slid to a stop.

"What's wrong, Brenda?" Ima asked.

She bolted from the ATV and ran back across the bridge. Donald followed and found her hunched over a stone wall.

"I am okay now," Brenda said. "The voices over there are deafening and saying such horrible things. I can walk back to the lodge by myself. Go find Abby, I'll be fine."

She stood up and brushed herself off.

"Be careful," she said then turned and walked towards the lodge.

Donald re-joined the others and they continued into the woods where a dark curtain of foliage surrounded them. Sound and light were muted and the air was flat and cold. Only Joseph saw the trail that Abby had left, a transparent vapor floating above the path.

"She is this way," he said steering the vehicle off the path.

They idled through the misty forest and found Abby lying in a pile of leaves. She wore a white nightgown and lay completely still. Joseph stopped the vehicle and all jumped out and ran to her. Ima knelt next to Abby to check her condition while Joseph removed leaves from her hair. Abby's eyes fluttered open and she plunged a knife into Joseph's side. Ima knocked Abby unconscious with the butt of her gun.

Donald helped Ima carry Joseph and Abby to the ATV where Ima applied pressure to Joseph's wound. Donald started the ATV and raced the vehicle back to the lodge.

"No hospital. Get us inside," Joseph said.

"You need a doctor," Ima insisted.

"A doctor can't help, get us inside," Joseph urged.

Ima and Donald carried Joseph into the great room and placed him on the floor in front of the fireplace.

"First aid kit," he said pointing towards the kitchen.

Ima sprang towards the kitchen and opened cabinets until she found the kit. Donald and Brenda struggled to carry Abby upstairs as she thrashed and fought to get free.

"I want her sedated and restrained," Ima called out. "Check the back of my truck for something to hold her, my keys are on the table," she added pointing towards the alcove.

Ima turned back to Joseph. She held a towel against his side and put pressure on the wound.

"Let me take a look," Ima said.

He raised his arm and exposed a two-inch puncture oozing blood.

"Just a flesh wound," he said with a weak smile.

Ima smiled back. He was a tough old guy. Living out here all these years had seen to that.

"Okay this is going to sting," she said.

She poured disinfectant on the wound and he stiffened and winced in pain.

"Sorry Joseph," she said.

"It's okay," he said with a nod.

She bandaged the wound and examined her work. As a deputy she received medical training but never had to use it before.

"We will have to change this every few hours," Ima said. "But I still want to get you to the hospital."

"Not safe," Joseph said. "You saw what happened to Terry."

CHAPTER THIRTY

Donald and Brenda walked down the staircase into the great room. Joseph rested under a plaid blanket with Ima at his side, the firelight created shadows on his weathered face.

"How is he doing?" Donald asked.

"Good, he's strong," Ima answered. "The bleeding has stopped and the knife didn't hit any major organs. He was lucky. The pocket of his jacket was full of stones which shielded him."

Ima held up the worn leather jacket, the pocket was torn and stained with blood.

"What about Abby?" Ima asked.

"She's okay," Donald said. "We handcuffed her to the bed and gave her a sedative. She's sleeping."

"Something has gotten to her," Brenda said. "Abby would never hurt anyone."

"So what now?" asked Ima.

Donald gestured towards the hallway. "We need to bury that thing and figure out what Calvin Smith was looking for. I'm going to the study to see what I can find."

"Ima?" Joseph called out weakly.

The fading light of the sun streamed through the back windows.

"Yes, Joseph," Ima answered.

"We need to prepare the house for the night," he said. "All of the doors and windows must be bolted shut and I need my bag." He tried to get up.

"Joseph, lay still. I'll get it," Ima said.

"It's against the wall. Thank you," he said weakly.

Ima brought the bag and sat next to him on the couch.

"Now tell me what to do," she said.

"Empty the contents on the table there," he said.

With Brenda's help, Ima organized the contents of Joseph's bag into three rows of stones, medallions and bags of herbs.

"It will be coming tonight," Joseph said. "We must be ready when it does. Secure this room by putting stones in a circle around the center of it. Between each stone sprinkle the herbs. Keep a medallion on each of you, and make sure to give one to Donald and Abby."

Ima went to work placing the stones and herbs around the room. The mix was pungent with specks of salt and green leaves. Brenda picked up a medallion then walked to the study and knocked on the mirror door.

"Come in," she heard Donald say.

She slid open the mirror and found Donald hunched over the desk. Books were strewn all around him. He wore horn-rim glasses and his brown hair was disheveled.

"Any luck?" she asked.

He answered slowly. "Well, yes. I now know what we need to find to stop the Raven Mocker."

"That's great," Ima exclaimed. "But what's wrong?"

"We are searching for a needle in a field of haystacks."

Upstairs, Ima put a medallion around Abby's neck. She was asleep with a bandage on her forehead. She felt bad about hitting her, but Abby had given her no choice. Turning to leave, she noticed a medallion similar to the ones Joseph had given them. It was lying in the window near Abby's bed. She hung the medallion on the window latch and saw something shine out in the woods. It looked like a signal.

Ima went downstairs and made her way past a sleeping Joseph and into the kitchen. She found the binoculars and trained them on the woods where a woman stood at the tree line. She turned on a flashlight then stepped outside and walked across the field behind the lodge. The woman stood on the far side of the bridge holding an object that glimmered in the beam of the light.

Ima called out, "You there. I am a police officer. Please identify yourself."

The woman swayed back and forth but said nothing. Ima walked across the bridge and trained her light on the woman. It was Abby, dressed in white, holding her medallion. She held it front of her face and stared at it as it spun on its chain. Ima holstered her weapon and walked over to her.

"Abby, what are you doing out here?" she asked.

When she stepped off the bridge the darkness enveloped her.

"Abby help me," she said.

Ima fell to her knees fighting to breathe as Abby glided towards her with crimson patches appearing on her white dress. Her arms were covered with gashes and her face was smashed and distorted. Ima had seen these types of injuries working the highway patrol. The creature reached down and stroked her hair as if to comfort her. Then it yanked her head back and lifted her off the ground.

"No," Ima managed to choke out.

The smell of rotting flesh and burned skin hit Ima as she was pulled forward. She aimed her gun and fired but the weapon only sounded a muted click. She pulled the medallion from her pocket and the creature released her. She fell back onto the hard stones of the bridge and let the cold air pour back into her lungs. The creature moved to the edge of the bridge and locked dead eyes on her.

"What the fuck?" Ima shouted and ran back to the lodge.

She ran in the back door of the lodge and bolted it behind her then stumbled into the great room and found Donald and Brenda waiting with Joseph.

"Ima, where have you been?" Joseph asked.

"Out back, something horrible has happened to Abby. She's in the woods–" Ima stopped in mid-sentence.

Abby sat in an armchair in the corner of the room, eating a bowl of soup. Her ankle was cuffed to the leg of the chair. The medallion dangled from her neck as she leaned forward to spoon the soup.

"I am feeling much better now, Ima," she said slowly.

"Maybe you saw my sister Addie. She lives in the forest now." Abby smiled a medicated smile.

Ima sat on the floor in front of the fireplace and explained the details of her encounter in the woods.

"Ima, I told you not to leave this lodge. No one is to leave this house," Joseph said.

"I'm sorry," Ima said dejected.

"Let's go get you cleaned up," Brenda said.

She took Ima's hand and led her upstairs.

"Donald, please go down to the cavern were we left the remains," Joseph said. "Soak some of that gauze in the water." He gestured toward the first aid kit. "The waters have recuperative powers. It might help the bump on Abby's head, and this hole in my side."

"Of course," Donald said.

Donald walked into the hallway and unhooked a kerosene lantern from the wall. He lit the lantern and slipped into the opening behind the mirror. The lantern light glowed on the gray walls of the cavern. The tarp with its horrible cargo lay where they had left it, the nylon stained black with its oozing contents.

Donald approached the water and placed the lantern on a stone ledge. Mist swirled over the surface and danced in the yellow light. He dipped the gauze and sealed it in a plastic bag. He shot a nervous glance at the tarp, then walked up the stone steps and returned to the great room. Ima sat across from Brenda who was feeding Joseph. Abby was slumped over sleeping in a chair by the fire.

"Feeling okay?" Donald asked Ima.

"Yes, feeling human again."

"It could have been worse," Joseph cautioned. "Much worse."

"What was that thing? The Raven Mocker?" Ima asked.

"Yes," Joseph answered. "The Raven Mocker can take the form of any animal or person it has encountered."

But why would it imitate Abby?" Brenda asked.

"It wasn't imitating Abby. It was imitating her sister," Joseph answered.

"The creature has a hold over Abby and is using tragic memories of her sister. It will use any advantage it can to manipulate and destroy us. Your family has fallen prey to this beast and anyone associated with your family will be used or destroyed until it is satisfied."

Joseph noticed that Donald had brought the dampened gauze. "Ima, could you dress Abby's wound with that gauze?" Joseph asked.

"Mine too, if you please."

"Sure," Ima answered.

Donald handed her the bag. Joseph spoke as Ima changed his bandage.

"When I was a young boy I was bitten by a rattlesnake. I was foraging in the forest with my grandfather when I stepped on the snake. I became dizzy and began to vomit, but we were too far into the woods to get to a doctor. Instead, my grandfather carried me to the lake behind us." Joseph gestured towards the back of the lodge. "I remember he walked into the water carrying me. By that point I could barely move, I was dying. When we entered the water I felt a surge of energy and the effects of the venom disappeared. However, the cure did not come free. My grandfather had aged noticeably by the time we dried off. The water needed to draw power in order to heal me and my grandfather was the only living thing around."

"What about this?" Ima said holding up the remaining gauze.

"It is safe. There are five of us here and we are not asking much of the water," Joseph answered.

CHAPTER THIRTY ONE

R ain began to patter on the metal roof of the lodge then quickly intensified into a hail storm. Chunks of ice hit the stone veranda and bounced wildly in every direction. The wind whipped across the field and uprooted trees behind the lodge, beyond the bridge the forest was untouched by the storm. Brenda joined Donald at the window.

"A bad storm is coming," Donald said looking out the kitchen window.

The lights flickered off and the lodge was plunged into darkness.

"Shit, power's out," Ima said in the other room.

The light from the fireplace cast leaping shadows throughout the lodge. Donald located a flashlight in a kitchen drawer and gave it to Brenda.

"Thanks."

"We better get back to the others," he said.

They returned to the great room and found Joseph sitting in front of the fire. Abby sat nearby and stared into the flames.

"It is upon us," Joseph said looking into the fire. "We need to be ready."

He lifted his shirt and removed the dressing on his wound, then crossed the room and removed Abby's. Both of their wounds were completely healed with no evidence of scarring.

"It's cold in here, I'm going to check the furnace," Donald said.

"I would not recommend that," Joseph said. "The only access is from the outside and no one should leave this room. You can find blankets in that closet." Joseph pointed at a set of double doors.

Donald walked to the closet, and retrieved an arm-load of blankets and pillows.

"Might as well be comfortable," he said.

"Yes," Joseph replied. "We have plenty of wood and supplies, and if things get really bad, we can go down here."

He rolled back a Persian rug and revealed a trap door in the floor, then pulled a lever and opened the metal door.

"Ted believed in being prepared," Joseph said.

Ima shined her flashlight down the black opening in the floor. A metal ladder ran down the wall.

"What is it?" Ima asked.

"The building's keep," Joseph answered.

"Think of it as a safe room. Go on down and have a look. I will watch Abby," said Joseph.

Ima climbed down the ladder as Donald trained the flashlight on the floor below. She found a hand-cranked generator and powered on the lights. The bulbs flickered for a moment then burned brightly. The room was windowless and made of steel with bunks built into the walls. Symbols were painted across the walls and ceiling. Donald and Brenda followed her down into the room.

"All the comforts of home," Donald said. "Your uncle didn't leave anything to chance, Brenda."

The trap door closed above them.

"What the hell," Ima said.

Ima climbed the ladder and tried to open the door. It wouldn't move. She pounded on the door.

"Joseph, let us out of here," she said.

Joseph's muffled voice came from above. "I am sorry, Ima. I cannot."

"Joseph!" She banged harder.

"It is for your own good. The creature can imitate any of us, you saw that for yourself," Joseph said through the locked door.

"Joseph!" Ima screamed pounding harder and harder, but there was only silence now.

He placed the rug back over the trap door and examined the perimeter of the stone circle. The rain continued to pound the roof of the lodge and the wind caused the building to creak. Abby stared expressionless at Joseph with blood dripping down her manacled ankle from scraping the handcuff up and down the wooden leg of the chair.

The air was freezing cold and Joseph could now see his breath. He walked to the fireplace and added a log to the fire, then wrapped a blanket around Abby's shoulders.

Behind the lodge, trees cracked and fell into the surging river and broken trunks jutted from the water. Joseph walked to the kitchen window and watched the storm rage outside then dashed through the great room and into the hallway as Abby cackled behind him.

"She's coming Joseph, she coming," Abby screamed.

In the great room, a gust of wind blew down the chimney, forcing ash and burning embers into the air. The fire roared as the cold air rushed over the logs and Abby grinned as the ash formed into the shape of an old woman with burning embers for eyes. The creature floated along the hearth and stopped at the stone circle. Abby gazed adoringly at the creature which extended an ashen hand to her. She stood and moved towards the fireplace dragging the heavy chair behind her. The stones and herbs were swept away when she walked out of the circle. Abby contorted when the creature embraced her and buried its burning embers into her eyes.

Joseph stood on the steps to the cavern floor when the wind howled and slammed the mirror shut behind him. He shined his flashlight into the dark and walked down the steps.

"No," Joseph said.

The channel was nearly drained with only puddles of water remaining and the tarp was ripped open with black stones scattered around the floor. Behind him, sharp claws scraped on stone. He spun and saw a raven perched on the steps. His light passed through the bird illuminating the door behind it. It made a guttural sound and spread its wings until its shadow touched the walls, then closed and encircled him. His arms were pinned at his sides forcing the flashlight from his shaking hand. The creature forced him to the ground and began to peck into his chest. Joseph began to scream, its vengeance would be slow this time.

CHAPTER THIRTY TWO

"We need to get the stones and the remains back to where this all started. Somewhere around the cabin they missed collecting a stone," Donald said. "After Calvin and his men attacked the creature, they were supposed to count the stones and gather them all up. They rushed the job and missed one."

Ima sat on a lower bunk within the keep. The fluorescent light cast a greenish glow on the metal walls.

"How are we going to find an old cabin, much less a single stone in the middle of a forest?" Ima asked.

"I have a map," Donald said tapping the front pocket of his jacket. "A map to the cabin at least. The stones they used were black hematite which wasn't common to the area."

"But how do we get out of here?" Brenda asked.

"There's a fire axe hanging on the wall there," Donald said pointing towards the ladder. "The frame around the hatch is wood. It may take a while, but I think we can chop our way out."

They all jumped to their feet when the trap door swung open above them.

"Joseph?" Donald called out.

Abby climbed down with only the back of her legs visible, a pair of handcuffs attached to a broken chair leg dangled from her ankle.

"Abby, thank goodness," Brenda said.

Abby reached the floor of the keep and grabbed the axe from the wall, then turned and knocked the generator to the floor. The lights flickered as the damaged generator pulsed. She advanced toward them with burnt cavities where her eyes had been. The room went dark and they scrambled when she swung and hit the wall near Ima's head. The lights came on and Donald and Brenda were able to run to the base of the ladder. Ima waved for them to escape then wrenched the axe from Abby's grip and swung it into her throat. Abby collapsed forward and drove the pointed backside of the axe through Ima's heart. Donald watched helplessly as the two woman died impaled together on the axe. Brenda and Donald climbed out of the keep and into the wind that howled through the broken windows of the lodge. The smoldering logs in the fireplace cast a dim glow on the destruction. Donald grabbed Brenda's hand and ran towards the study and when they entered the hallway, she stopped in front of the mirror.

"What is it?" he yelled over the wind.

"I thought I heard Joseph," Brenda answered.

He looked around and noticed the mirror door in the hallway.

"Wait here," he said.

Donald slipped inside, crept down the stairs and found Joseph lying on his back with his arms pinned at his sides. His blood stained shirt was ripped open and a black bird stood on his chest. Donald reached into his pocket, retrieved his medallion, and then wrapped the chain around the bird. The creature let out a cry, then flew into the wall leaving only black vapor behind. Donald knelt down and helped Joseph to his feet.

"I'm alright. We need the stones and remains," Joseph said.

Donald gathered the stones and placed them into the tarp while the wisps of black vapor reorganized into a swirling mass.

"Hurry!" Joseph shouted struggling to climb the steps.

Donald tied the tarp and dragged it out the doorway behind Joseph.

"Close the door," Donald yelled to Brenda.

Brenda closed the door just before a tremendous force struck it. The impact shattered the mirror sending shards of glass into the hallway. The wood behind the mirror was intact, but damaged, with wisps of black vapor pouring through the cracks. They all ran down the hallway and into the study.

"Make a circle, use the stones," Joseph said pointing to the tarp.

Brenda and Donald placed the black stones around the wood floor of the study and climbed inside the circle with Joseph. The wound on his chest was fading away.

"Where is Abby and Ima?" Joseph asked.

Donald paused before answering. "They are both dead," he said finally.

"That thing took hold of Abby and made her do terrible things," Brenda said staring at the ground with tears in her eyes.

"We will see to them when this is over. I am sorry," Joseph said.

"So, what now?" Brenda asked.

"We need to finish it," Joseph answered.

The air in the study turned cold and a hard blow struck the door.

"It has found us, we must go now!" Joseph yelled. "Help me gather these up," he said grabbing the circle of stones.

Joseph opened the closet door and pushed in the panel to the corridor behind it.

"This way," Joseph said voice rising in fear.

They rushed through the corridor and out into the woods as the creature broke through the door and entered the study. The hail had turned into a cold pelting rain and the wind whipped through the trees. When they reached the ATV, Joseph slid across the wet vinyl seat and started the engine. Donald swung the tarp into the back then helped Brenda into the vehicle.

CHAPTER THIRTY THREE

The wind ripped at the ATV's canvas top and its headlights revealed downed trees scattered like matchsticks. Joseph accelerated onto the bridge as the creature wailed behind them. The bridge collapsed as they crossed, plunging their vehicle into the surging water. The ATV remained afloat, but spun wildly as Joseph fought to regain control.

"Hold on," Joseph shouted above the storm.

Brenda tightened her grip on the roll bar and Donald wrapped his arm around the tarp. They shot through a narrow section of the river and slammed into a downed oak, ripping the hood off the vehicle. Rushing water filled the ATV and stalled the engine, and then the headlights dimmed and went out.

They passed the tributary to the lodge which was blocked with downed trees and debris. The current slowed and they were left spinning downstream where the ruined vehicle came to a rest on a muddy bank a mile into the forest.

"We better move," Joseph said.

Climbing out of the wreckage, Donald managed to drag the water logged tarp onto the shore. Joseph opened a watertight hatch and pulled out two jackets, a flashlight and a blanket, thankfully still dry. He handed the blanket to Brenda who was shivering violently.

"Where is that thing?" Donald asked.

"Back on the other side, I hope," Joseph answered. "The river crossing should have slowed it, but it will find us soon enough. We need to go."

Donald studied the wet map with a yellow flashlight.

Joseph paced nervously. "Which way?" he asked.

"Follow me," Donald said.

Donald and Joseph each pulled a corner of the tarp and dragged the load behind them. They walked until they reached a fork in the path.

"Left," Donald said.

The turn led them down a narrow trail running parallel to a creek. Joseph stopped abruptly. A pair of vultures stood on the far bank.

"What's the matter, Joseph?" Donald asked.

Joseph answered, "Nothing is wrong." I just need to rest a moment."

Brenda struggled to block the distractions, but the voices grew louder and images of horrible things illuminated like flashbulbs in the dark. She stared down at the ground and fought the urge to react. They reached a bridge that crossed the creek. The bridge was a rusted red skeleton overgrown with vines with its wooden planks all but gone.

"We need to cross here," Donald said hesitantly.

Donald stepped on the bridge to test its strength. "Seems solid enough."

Donald walked across a girder with Joseph following a few steps behind him. Brenda stepped on to the bridge, the water below her began to churn and skeletal hands emerged from the creek. She took a step forward and a spectral hand brushed her foot sending a wash of cold over it.

"Brenda, hurry!" Donald shouted.

The Raven Mocker, in the form of an old woman with black eyes and pallid skin, appeared behind her and closed quickly. Brenda ran along the beam trying to block out the distractions and was halfway across when she lost her balance and disappeared under the surface of the water. Donald and Joseph ran to the creek bank looking for her, while the Raven Mocker leered down from the bridge. The creek began to bubble and Brenda was lifted by misty hands to the waters edge where Donald was able to carry her out.

"Look," Joseph said.

The Raven Mocker wrestled against an unseen force and thrashed in rage as if bound. Brenda opened her eyes and said, "What happened?"

Donald got her to her feet and wrapped his jacket around her.

"Brenda, we need to go. Are you okay to walk?" Donald asked.

"I'm okay."

The Raven Mocker's screams of rage filled the woods behind them.

CHAPTER THIRTY FOUR

"There it is," Donald said pointing towards a triple oak.

The map indicated a trail behind the tree that led to the cabin.

"Can I see the map?" Joseph asked.

"Sure," Donald answered handing the map to Joseph.

"We are close," Joseph said. "We need to pass through the town of Culver."

"Culver?" Donald asked.

"Yes. It was a settler's town deep in the mountains. The people of Culver refused to leave when these lands were abandoned and they were never heard from again," Joseph answered. "No one ever dared to look for them."

"Should we find another way?" Donald asked.

"No, on the contrary," Joseph said. "I am hoping the town of Culver can assist us."

Donald led Joseph and Brenda into a gorge where stones slid underfoot as they climbed down the steep grade.

"Careful," Donald said.

When they reached the bottom, they were surrounded by high stone walls and dead trees.

"This way," Donald said.

Down the trail was an abandoned farmhouse covered in vines with a crumbling barn behind it. The property was quiet and still, unoccupied for generations. Joseph stopped walking and rubbed his lower back.

"Joseph, do you need to stop and rest a minute?" Donald asked.

"No," Joseph said. "I am fine. We must go on."

A bluff overlooked the town of Culver which consisted of six gray buildings surrounded by scrub land. Culver Lake was visible behind the town. Donald dragged the tarp into town then sat in the dirt road and waited for Joseph and Brenda to catch up.

"I need to rest a moment," Donald said.

"Yes, of course," Joseph answered.

"We need to spend a few minutes here anyway. Can you stay out here and keep watch?" Joseph asked.

"Sure, where are you going?" Donald asked.

"In there," Joseph said pointing at the hulking ruin of a hotel.

"I better go with you, it's not safe," Donald said.

"No," Joseph replied. "Please do as I ask."

"Okay," Donald said with a nod. He walked over to the crumbing steps of the hotel and sat down. "I will be right here."

"Thank you," Joseph said.

"Brenda?" Joseph gestured towards the doors of the hotel.

Brenda followed Joseph into the building and entered the lobby. The hotel was ravaged by time with moldy paintings on its walls and a rack full of tattered coats in the corner. Joseph trained his flashlight across the room, while Brenda stared at the floor and tried to handle the flood of distractions.

"We need to understand what happened here. It may show us the best way to fight the beast," Joseph said. "I need you to open your mind to this place and tell me what you see."

They were in a tomb, with crumbled skeletons on a rotted velvet couch and bones scattered down the staircase and across the front desk. Behind it, were the remains of the last survivors trying to reach a dozen rifles still propped against the wall.

"These people were ambushed," Brenda whispered.

She turned to face the room and opened her mind. Dozens of images played out before her, she had never seen so many at one time.

"Ravens," she said aloud. "Dozens of them. They killed everyone."

She saw the monstrous birds plunge their beaks into the chests of the townspeople. Black feathers dripped in blood as they swallowed the hearts of their victims.

"What else can you see?" Joseph asked.

"It looks like they were gathered for a meeting. The entire town was here," she answered.

Joseph walked behind the front desk.

"They were assembling a cache of weapons," she said. "Planning to stop it."

Joseph studied the walls of the room.

"Not a shot was fired," he said.

"There was no time," Brenda added. "They were attacked too quickly. Where did they all come from?" She asked.

"They were all the same creature split into parts," Joseph answered.

Donald jumped to his feet when they walked out of the hotel.

"You okay?" he asked them.

Brenda nodded. She looked dazed.

"Yes," Joseph answered. "We better get moving again."

"I have been studying the map. We need to follow the lake for a few miles," Donald said. The cabin should be on the eastern shore."

They left the rotted memory of the town and walked onto a trail that circled the lake where whispers in the mist echoed across the surface of the water.

CHAPTER THIRTY FIVE

The cabin stood alone with a ring of scorched earth around it, the smell in the air was foul when Joseph stepped onto the burnt soil.

"Wait," he said, hand raised towards them.

He walked forward holding the medallion that hung from his neck, then entered the front door and disappeared into the cabin. Donald and Brenda waited anxiously as the minutes passed. Joseph finally emerged and waved them forward.

"Brenda, I need you to look for Calvin Smith," Joseph said.

She turned in a circle and concentrated.

"Over there," she said pointing towards the front porch. "That is where it happened."

She approached the porch and saw men standing in front of the cabin. They were throwing stones at an old woman, only it wasn't an old woman. Her black eyes glared at the men like a wild animal. Calvin hit the woman first. Brenda watched the scene play over again.

"I see him," she said. "I see Calvin."

"Brenda, watch where the stone that Calvin throws lands," Donald said.

She watched again.

"It went under the house," she said. "Right there," she added pointing at a jagged gap in the stone foundation of the building.

Donald crawled onto his knees and shined his flashlight into the opening, a single hematite stone sat in the dirt under the cabin.

"I see it, but I can't reach it," Donald said.

"We need to get under there," Joseph said.

Donald tried, but couldn't fit into the opening.

"I'll go," Brenda said. "I'm the only one that will fit."

She crawled through the jagged opening and pushed her flashlight ahead of her.

"How are you doing?" Donald asked. He stood over the opening ready to pull her out.

"Good. Almost there," she answered.

The stench made it hard for her to breathe.

"I have it," she said.

"Brenda, toss the stone out the opening," Joseph said.

Brenda did and the stone skipped across the ground, Joseph grabbed it and placed it in the tarp with the others.

"I'm going to pull you out," Donald said.

"Okay," she answered.

She turned to grab her flashlight and was met with black eyes and the stench of rot. The Raven Mocker wrapped its claws around her hair and pulled her completely under the cabin.

"Brenda!" Donald shouted. "Help me Joseph, I've lost her!"

The two men reached into the opening as Brenda's screams filled the crawl space.

"I have her," Joseph said.

They pulled her out and turned her over, her body was limp and the front of her shirt was covered with blood. The creature crawled out through the opening and fell to the ground. The creature writhed in pain and changed becoming more bird-like, then spewed black liquid onto the ground.

In the pool of liquid was Brenda's heart, Joseph leaped forward and grabbed the lifeless organ.

"Help me get her to the water!" Joseph shouted.

They ran to the lake as the Raven Mocker languished on the ground with black eyes rolled back in its head. When they reached the water, they placed Brenda's body on the ground.

"Donald, go get the tarp and throw it into the water," Joseph said.

Donald ran to the cabin and found the Raven Mocker crawling to its feet. He grabbed the tarp and dragged it to the water where Brenda kneeled over Joseph and wept. He had aged dramatically and his breathing was labored. The heart donated to Brenda two decades earlier lay lifeless at the edge of the lake. The water and Joseph's sacrifice had returned Brenda's own heart to her. Donald dragged the tarp into the water letting it sink to the depths of the lake and then ran to Joseph's side.

"Help me get him to the water," Donald said.

"No," Joseph said weakly. "The sands of time have run out for me. Leave me, I am where I belong."

He coughed and fought for another breath.

"Go now and never return," Joseph said.

His thin stick of an arm pointed past the cabin, then he gasped for air and was gone. Donald stood and put his arm around Brenda who was wet and shaking from the cold, but finally free of her distractions. A light breeze blew across the lake and sunlight streamed through the trees. Black feathers and ash blew across the ground and the Raven Mocker was no more.

THE SPINNING WHEEL

CHAPTER ONE

Tommy Roberts loved to play with building blocks and most afternoons you could find him splayed out across the floor working on a new project, but this day he was working on something new and quite unusual.

Casey, his old yellow lab, lay patiently by his side observing the progress of the shiny colored blocks. John Roberts sat on a tattered plaid sofa reading the newspaper while his son played. John looked up from his paper when a light breeze blew the wind chimes hanging on his porch. The sound reminded him of a tune from years past. He concentrated, but he couldn't pick out the melody.

"Damndest thing," he muttered to no one in particular, then went back to reading the local sports page.

The Milton Mights, the local minor league baseball team, were playing tomorrow night. He and his son enjoyed attending the games and Tommy would cheer loudly no matter which team got a hit.

It was just John and Tommy and Casey these days. His wife Mary called them her boys. That was before the cancer caught up with her two years ago. John buried Mary after 46 good years and one really bad one. They visited the place Tommy called the park once a week to put flowers on her grave, but Tommy didn't really understand. He was 44 years old with Down's syndrome and had the sweet mind of a six year old child.

John walked across the living room to see what his son was building. Tommy had been oddly quiet all morning and hadn't spoken since breakfast. Casey was asleep with his legs kicking softly in a dream. John peered over Tommy's shoulder and was shocked by the sight of an elaborate carousel built from plastic blocks. The carousel, over three feet in diameter, spun slowly as if moved by an unseen hand.

John bent, knees cracking, to examine the intricate details. Plastic horses moved up and down as the carousel spun. His son had never built anything like it.

"Daddy, you like?" Tommy asked.

"Why yes, Tommy boy. It's wonderful," he answered. "But where did you get it?"

"I make it Daddy," Tommy said. "All by myself."

"But son, where did you learn how to build this?"

"Mr. Adams," Tommy said with a grin.

"Mr. Adams?" John asked. "Does he work at your school?

"No Daddy. Mr. Adams under bed," Tommy answered.

Strange, John thought. Tommy never mentioned imaginary friends before.

"Come, I show you," Tommy said rising slowly to his feet.

Tommy looked older than 44, gray and almost entirely bald. He was plagued by many of the same health issues as John, who was 35 years his senior. John stood and followed Tommy upstairs to his room. Tommy had lived in the same room for four decades. The blue carpeting was worn and frayed and he still had the lamp with trains painted on it he had loved since he was a child. Tommy's room was a fading snapshot of a life caught in time.

Tommy struggled onto his hands and knees, pulled up the bed ruffle and said, "See Daddy."

With a groan, John joined his son on the floor and then peered under the bed. He saw something in the dark underneath the bed and heard distant music, the same melody he had heard earlier.

Tommy stood up and said, "See Daddy. Where Mr. Adams lives."

"Tommy, flip on the light, will you son?" John said wiping his eyes.

"But Mr. Adams go away," Tommy answered.

"That's okay, Tommy," John said. "Turn on the lights, please."

With the lights on, he discovered a collection of plastic block creations, all as elaborate as the carousel.

John climbed back to his feet and caught his breath.

"Tommy. Tell me again, where did you get all of these things?" John asked.

Tommy looked disappointed. "Daddy, Tommy built them. Built them all." Tommy was starting to get upset. Tears welled in his eyes.

"Calm down, son. I just wanted to know where you learned how to build it. You did a great job."

Tommy wiped a tear away and said, "Mr. Adams."

Tommy pointed at the ruffled bed.

"Okay, Tommy Boy. How about an ice cream?"

"Mulligan's?" Tommy asked.

"Sure, at Mulligan's. "Go get your coat on and we'll take a drive," John said.

CHAPTER TWO

John backed the tired Dodge wagon out his driveway. The air was cool but the sun shined brightly. Tommy was busy playing with a plastic figure with a black top hat.

"Who's your friend? John asked.

"Mr. Adams," Tommy answered softly.

He was twirling the figure between his fingers.

"Oh, that's the mysterious Mr. Adams," John said.

Tommy stayed quiet on the drive into Milton. Most of the leaves had fallen from the trees and the mountains loomed in the distance. John and his wife had discovered the town accidently years before. They were on a road trip, took a wrong turn and ended up in Milton. Ten years ago they decided to retire to the little town they found all those years before.

Tommy got excited when he saw the Milton downtown in the valley below them. The town had seen better times, but was holding its own.

"Ice cream," Tommy said pointing at the sign hanging over Mulligan's.

Tommy couldn't read, but recognized the faded sign shaped like an ice cream cone.

"Almost there, Tommy Boy," John answered.

John drove into an empty spot in front of the shop.

"They saved a spot for us."

"Yes, Daddy."

A bell clanged against the wooden door when John and Tommy entered the shop. The shopkeeper, Ed Clarkson, greeted them with a grin.

"Tommy, I think you ate up all the ice cream the last time you was in," Ed said.

"No," Tommy said. "There ice cream."

Mr. Clarkston feigned surprise and said, "So it is. You must have left a little!"

"I want some," Tommy said, ignoring Mr. Clarkston's comments.

"Tommy?" John asked with a frown.

"Please, I want some," Tommy corrected pointing at a tub of Neapolitan.

"Coming right up, sir," Mr. Clarkston replied. "John, cup of coffee? Just brewed a fresh pot."

"Sure, Ed. How can I turn that down?" John answered.

John sat with Tommy on a bench outside the shop. Dozens of initials had been carved into the bench over the years. He took a sip of coffee and looked at his son who was carefully eating an ice cream cone. He had always been a neat and precise boy despite his challenges. Maybe that is how he built the carnival pieces from the plastic blocks? Could he have some unrealized gift? Tommy finished his cone and threw his napkin in a trash can.

"Ready to go, Tommy? John asked. It's getting kinda late."

"Yes Daddy, all done," Tommy answered.

The sun was starting to set behind the mountains, the remaining leaves of the oak trees glowed a brilliant reddish gold.

CHAPTER THREE

John awoke the next morning to find Tommy hard at work. Plastic blocks were strewn all around him and Casey, sound asleep, manned his usual post next to him. The snores of the old dog were the only sounds in the room. There was a half-finished bowl of cereal on the floor. John walked around to see what Tommy was so busy doing and stopped suddenly. On the floor in front of Tommy sat a grand carnival entrance complete with ticket booths. Strands of Christmas lights surrounded a parking lot filled with plastic cars. A line of plastic people waited patiently for tickets. John rubbed the sleep from his eyes and focused on the incredible detail of Tommy's creation.

"Tommy how–" he stopped mid-sentence. "How are you building these things?"

"Mr. Adams," Tommy said with a smile.

Tommy held up the plastic figure with the black top hat. John was alarmed and thought to call Tommy's doctor.

"Doctor, oh no," he said aloud and then looked at his watch.

He remembered he had an appointment himself in forty minutes. He picked up the phone and called Betty Stewart, their next-door neighbor who was kind enough to watch Tommy on occasion.

"Hello, John," Betty answered. "I was about to call you. You did say Thursday at eight a.m.?"

"Yes," he said. "Running a little late."

"Be right over," Betty said.

He thanked Betty and hung up the phone then hurried upstairs to get ready. Betty was sitting in the living room when he came back down.

"Thanks again, Betty. I owe you one."

"You owe me more than one," Betty said with a laugh.

John put the car into gear and the transmission whined as he backed out of the driveway. John hurried into town already a few minutes late. Dr. Alvin Carter was a good egg and it would give him something to rib John about. They spent many Sundays together fly fishing the local rivers. He stopped at Amelia's Café to pick up two coffees, a peace offering for the good doctor. When he arrived, Carlene, Alvin's receptionist, was waiting for him.

"Morning, John," she said. "He's ready for you. Go right in."

John found Alvin sitting behind his desk.

"John, come in," Alvin said. "Please have a seat," he added closing his office door.

"Wow, Alvin. Giving me the official treatment this morning? Sorry I'm late," John said handing Alvin a coffee.

"Thanks John."

Alvin sat down and placed his coffee in front of him untouched.

"John," Alvin began. "We have been friends for a long time, so I am going to give it to you straight. The tests we performed on you a week ago did not turn out well."

"What are you talking about, Alvin?" He had never seen Alvin so serious before.

"John, I noticed some changes in you the last few months, so I ordered some tests. Do you remember we discussed it the last time you were in?"

"Sure," John lied.

He scarcely remembered anything about his last visit.

"John, you have Alzheimer's," Alvin said.

"You mean Old Timers, don't you pal?" John managed a weak grin.

Alvin continued speaking. "We need to get you on a regimen of medicines that can help slow this thing down."

What do you mean slow it down?" John asked.

"John, there is no cure," Alvin said. "We can only postpone the effects of the disease."

"Slow down for how long?" John said voice cracking. "Tommy needs me."

"John. At best you will have a few years, one or two living independently." Alvin cleared his throat. "You need to make arrangements for Tommy as soon as possible, while you are still capable."

Alvin stood up from behind his desk.

"Let me drive you home," Alvin said.

I am perfectly fine to drive myself," John answered quietly. "I got here, didn't I?"

John left Alvin's office closing the door behind him.

On the drive home, he passed Marconi's Liquor Store and thought about stopping. His drinking had gotten bad when Mary fell ill, but he promised to quit and focus on Tommy. What would he do now? He had no family left to speak of, and all of his friends were too old to take on Tommy. He couldn't end up in Oak Hurst. The place was unfit for the living. He and Mary had visited the facility years before, and found it dark and melancholy with the patients housed like medicated zombies.

The cold air whistled past a broken window vent as he drove home. He turned up the heat, the old car's heater still worked well enough to toast bread. He put the car in neutral and coasted around the last bend before his house. Tommy always loved coasting, so John would let the car roll down the hill and up the driveway. He rolled halfway up and put the car in park, then took a deep breath and prepared himself. Tommy was very perceptive to John's feelings and he didn't want to alarm him.

CHAPTER FOUR

"Hey, Tommy Boy. What's happening?" John said as he walked into the living room.

Betty was sleeping on the couch. Casey was sleeping at her feet.

"Hi, Daddy," Tommy said.

The entire living room floor was covered in plastic block buildings, cars and people. It was an incredible site that stretched to the kitchen door. The rides were moving and the park was brilliantly lit. Tiny block people congregated everywhere. The black plastic hat of Mr. Adams shined under an unseen spotlight at the center of the carnival.

John shook Betty's shoulder.

"Daddy, you like?" Tommy asked.

"I do son, I do," John answered.

Betty woke with a start and looked dazed for a few seconds.

"Oh, my goodness," she said. "Did I fall asleep? Is everything okay?"

"Yes, everything is fine," John said.

Betty put on a pair of glasses hanging around her neck.

"Sakes alive," she exclaimed. "Where did this all come from?"

"Betty, I built it. I built it all," Tommy said proudly.

"But, how?" she asked, looking alarmed and turning to John. "How long was I sleeping?"

"Not long, I've only been gone for an hour or so," John answered. "Can I speak with you for a minute? In the kitchen?"

Betty followed John into the kitchen.

"Betty, I am very concerned," John said.

"I'm sorry. I just dozed off," she answered.

"That's not what I meant," John said. "I am concerned about Tommy."

"Did anyone come in while I was gone?" John asked.

Betty looked flustered.

"Not that I was aware of," she answered. "But someone must have brought him all of that," she said.

"Yes, I realize that," John said. "This has been going on for the past few days and I haven't seen anyone. Tommy tells me he is building it all."

"It is not like Tommy to lie," Betty said.

"I know that," John replied.

They walked back into the living room and the oak kitchen door swung shut behind them.

"Look, Daddy. I built a ball park where Mights play baseball," Tommy said.

The stadium was built entirely of black plastic blocks and it stretched across the entry way to the front door.

"This was not here when I came in," John said.

"No, it wasn't," Betty agreed. Her voice was strained.

John's mind reeled as he studied the stadium.

"Must be a thousand black blocks right there," John said pointing at the stadium.

He looked across the room at Betty.

"He just has the one set of blocks. One set."

John stepped over the stadium and checked the front door. It was locked.

"Why is the stadium black," Betty asked John.

"Nighttime Betty, lights don't work no more," Tommy answered.

"Why don't the light work? Betty asked.

"Lights won't work on account of the lightning," Tommy answered.

"Oh, I see," Betty said looking confused.

John said, "Betty, maybe you could leave us alone."

"Sure, John. If you need anything, I'm right next door." Betty maneuvered past the stadium to the front door.

John sat down on his well-worn couch. He had forgotten about his visit with Alvin this morning, but the feelings of panic and helplessness returned. He watched his grown son play on the floor with Casey beside him, and picked up a white envelope sitting on the coffee table. The envelope contained two tickets to the baseball game with a picture of Grantham field printed on them. The picture of the stadium was identical to Tommy's creation looming in the entryway.

He felt his shirt pocket and pulled out the prescriptions Alvin wrote for him.

"Tommy Boy, let's take a ride to the drugstore," John said.

Tommy sat with his back to John, too busy to answer.

"Tommy?" John said again.

Tommy turned as if waking from a dream.

"Let's take a ride to the drug store," John said again.

"Okay, Daddy. We come home again fast. Mr. Adams needs carnival all done tonight," Tommy answered.

"He does, does he?" John said. "Well we better get moving then."

John got Tommy out the front door and on the way to Doc's Pharmacy. The clouds were painted with charcoal hues and the fallen leaves scattered as they drove along the country road to town. John didn't really understand what worry was until Alvin explained it to him this morning. The slide was inevitable and within a short time the quiet life he enjoyed with his son would be destroyed. Alvin had made that painfully clear. His social security and pension wouldn't pay for private care and Mary's illness had cost them their life's savings. He and Tommy would both be institutionalized. His would be a short stay but Tommy would be serving a life sentence in the grim state-run home.

He parked on a side street behind Doc's and got out of the car, then zipped Tommy's jacket up and braced against the cold air.

"There you go, Tommy Boy, no use catching a cold on the way to the pharmacy."

"Yes, Daddy."

Tommy always agreed and never gave John a minute of trouble. He simply enjoyed the moment he lived in.

"Hey, John. Tommy. How's your day going?" Henry asked.

Henry was behind the pharmacy counter stocking the shelves with the sleeves of his white coat rolled up.

"Hi, Henry." John handed him the prescriptions. "Need to pick these up."

"Sure thing, John." Henry read the prescriptions and left the counter without saying another word.

Tommy wandered the toy aisles examining the colorful boxes. A few minutes had passed when Henry returned from the back room. The prescriptions were stapled in neat white bags. He started to speak and stopped, looking sadly at Tommy.

"John, do you have any questions about your medication?"

"No, no I don't." John answered.

"Well, my home number's on the bag. Please do not hesitate to call if you need anything."

"I will. Thanks, Henry."

John and Tommy left the pharmacy and went to the car. Tommy walked like a man on a mission, which was quite unlike him. He usually liked to make the rounds while visiting the square. John looked up at the darkening sky.

"Might get rained out tonight, Tommy," John said.

Tommy stood next to the car and surveyed the sky.

"Yes, Daddy. We have lightning tonight," Tommy answered.

CHAPTER FIVE

Tommy went back to work on the carnival the moment they arrived home. John sat on the couch and switched on the local news, a reporter was covering a local event with a series of colorful tents being erected behind her. The camera panned out and John saw the sprawling carnival with its grounds decorated in elaborate lights and vintage rides from another time. Tommy's carnival on the floor of the living room was an exact replica of the image John saw on his Zenith.

He picked up the remote control and turned up the sound, the reporter was interviewing a man identified as R.G. Adams. The man wore a black tuxedo and top hat. His beard and moustache were waxed to perfect points, and he carried a cane with a silver handle.

Tommy turned to his father and said, "Mr. Adams, Daddy."

John watched intently as Adams opened his arms in an exaggerated gesture of welcome.

"Looks like some show, Tommy Boy," John said. "I guess you must have seen this on the news?"

"No, Daddy. Don't like news," Tommy answered.

The reporter appeared on the TV again. The caption read: MYSTERY CARNIVAL SURPRISES LOCAL AUTHORITIES.

John stood and switched the TV off, standing in the middle of the block carnival like a giant.

"What do you say we skip the game tonight and pay your Mr. Adams a visit?" John asked.

"Yes, Daddy," Tommy answered. "Game gonna be cancelled anyhow. On account of the lightning."

"Of course it is, Tommy," John said with a nod.

John looked at the black block stadium then picked up the phone and dialed.

"Hello, this is Darla, can I help you?"

"Hey, Darla, this is John Roberts. How you doin?" John asked.

"Just fine. How have you and Tommy been? Haven't sent y'all out at the park lately," Darla said.

"Well, we were planning to come out tonight, but we may end up going to that carnival instead," John said.

"Ain't that the strangest thing the way that carnival just blew into town?" Darla asked. "Just popped up overnight. No one even saw them drive in."

"Yes," John said hesitantly, looking at Tommy's carnival. "Strange it is. Darla, the reason I was calling was to see if the game was on tonight."

"So far," Darla answered. "But the sky is clouding up and the wind is swirling a bit. Looks like we might be in for some bad weather."

"Thanks," John said.

John hung up the phone and said, "Tommy, do you want to get going in a few minutes?"

Tommy looked up and said, "Sure, Daddy. All done now."

John stepped over the carnival and went up to his bedroom to change clothes. The closet he shared with Mary was still filled with her clothes. He freshened up and pulled a sweater over his head then picked up the bag containing his prescriptions. A "Living with Alzheimer's" flyer was tucked inside. He left the medicine unopened on the counter. He would start his decline tomorrow. Tonight he needed to understand the connection between his son and the odd carnival.

Tommy was waiting by the front door when he walked down the staircase. His eyes were alive and he had a broad smile on his face. Without a word they left and drove along Red Mountain Road towards the fairgrounds. The old Dodge's engine whined as they reached the top of the hill and the spectacle of the carnival unfolded below them. The lights of a spinning Ferris wheel cut through the darkness. John slowed and turned into an empty dirt parking lot as lightning flashed and illuminated a black sky.

"Better hurry, Tommy. We might get rained out," John said.

"Okay, Daddy," Tommy said.

They walked through the brilliant entrance of the carnival where thousands of tiny bulbs were strung along metal poles. The rides were spinning and twirling, but the carnival was empty.

Tommy began to run. "There, Daddy."

He pointed at an ornate carousel with a painted mosaic of an ancient ocean on its canopy. The carousel was polished to a mirror shine and wooden horses gleamed in the light of the moon. Tommy reached the carousel and climbed onto the back of a white horse trimmed in gold. John caught up to him and stopped to catch his breath.

"Tommy, not sure this ride's running," John said.

Tommy put his feet in the stirrups of his wooden steed. The painted eyes of his horse gleamed wildly. The lights suddenly illuminated and the brilliance of the carousel's detailing came alive. Each horse was hand carved and completely unique from the others. Gold leaf lined the walls and ceiling. John gazed around in awe at the splendor of the carousel.

"Quite a beauty, isn't she?"

John turned to find a black figure emerging from a door in the center of the carousel.

"Mr. Roberts, welcome," Mr. Adams said gesturing with a white gloved hand.

Mr. Adams was as impressive as the carousel. He wore a black velvet cloak and top hat and clutched the same silver cane John had seen on the television. He wore a ruby ring on his right hand and the gold of the ring glowed beneath the lights. He stared intently at John as he spoke.

"Mr. Roberts, I know you have questions."

"Well..."

Mr. Adams continued, "Life holds many questions does it not?"

His black boots clicked on the wooden floor of the carousel as he stepped in front of John.

"Do you ever wonder why one person dies in a car crash while another wins a lottery? Mr. Adams asked and paused momentarily. "Sometimes it is meant to be. But sometimes accidents can occur in the fabric of random things. Maybe the path of somebody's life turned right, when it should have turned left.

John sat stone-faced watching the exaggerated movements of the elegant man.

"Our job here," Mr. Adams said, "is to make corrections to these mistakes. Although we cannot undo these errors, we can make amends."

"What do you want from us?" John said softly.

"Actually, it is what you should want from me," Mr. Adams answered. "A series of mistakes have occurred in this town. You and your son have been the victims of these errors while others have received undeserved benefits. It is my job to set these matters straight."

Mr. Adams removed his hat and sat down on a seat across from John. His hair was long and black, and slicked against white skin.

"Mr. Roberts, I do not often tender choices in moments like these, but in this case I feel compelled to do so," Mr. Adams said.

"What type of choice?" John asked.

"You and you son are both faced with challenges. Tommy's challenge has been with him for a long time and yours is new to you," Mr. Adams answered.

"How do you know so much about us?" John asked.

Mr. Adams ignored the question and continued speaking.

"This evening I will offer you a choice."

Mr. Adams stood and placed a hand on Tommy's shoulder.

"I am prepared to take away Tommy's challenge," Mr. Adams said moving in front of John, slowly spinning his cane in his fingertips. "Or, I can take away yours."

Mr. Adams turned and walked to the small door in the center of the carousel and opened it. The circular room inside was empty and devoid of the gears and wires John expected to see. A solitary candle sat on a round table and illuminated the room.

"Return to me with your answer tomorrow night Mr. Roberts," Mr. Adams said, eyes gleaming in the darkness.

Mr. Adams turned and entered the circular room, and pinched out the candle with his gloved fingers. The door closed behind him and the lights faded off leaving them alone on the dark carousel with only the light of the moon washing over the still wooden horses.

On the drive home, Tommy acted as if he had awoken from a dream.

"Was fun, Daddy. We come tomorrow?"

"We'll see, Tommy," John said.

John flipped on the car's radio to clear his head.

"Tragedy has struck the town of Milton and one person is feared dead this evening when a fire broke out at the Milton Mights baseball stadium," the radio announcer said. "The victim is reported to be Frank Reynolds, the controversial winner of last year's Powerball lottery. Mr. Reynolds was the man with a history of domestic violence who won a fortune only weeks after his wife divorced him. Sources have reported an electrical storm in the area shortly before the start of the game. Thanks to the fast actions of the police, the estimated crowd of seven hundred was safely evacuated. The stadium, however, is considered a complete loss."

John turned the black plastic knob to shut off the radio and drove in silence. Rain began to fall and the wipers of the Dodge struggled to clear the water squeaking each time they made a pass. He pulled into his carport and sat for a moment listening to the sound of the rain then looked over at his son.

"Tommy, it's time to go to bed," John said softly.

John walked around the car and roused Tommy from a deep sleep. The rain fell harder as he fumbled for the key to the front door. He opened the door and turned on the foyer light. The living room floor was empty except for the spinning carousel.

CHAPTER SIX

T he next morning, John woke well after his usual six a.m. He focused blurry eyes on his alarm clock. Eleven forty-five a.m.

"What the hell," he muttered.

He rushed down the hallway, stopped at Tommy's doorway and found his son sleeping. He let him sleep and walked downstairs. The sun shined brightly through the living room windows and the carousel sat in a shadow cast by the coffee table. He kneeled to examine it. The toy had changed and was now the rudimentary creation of a child. He sat down on the couch and felt something he had been denied for years - hope.

After a long day of waiting, John was ready to bring Tommy back to the carnival. He had spent the day watching news coverage of the stadium disaster and could watch no more. He shut the television off and put on his jacket. It was 7:15 p.m. and already dark.

"Tommy, put on your jacket. We need to take a ride," John said.

"Okay, Daddy," Tommy answered.

Tommy didn't ask where they were going and maybe already knew. They stepped through a pelting rain and into the car. John cranked the starter and the wagon finally fired up. He wiped the windshield with a rag to clear the fog from the glass. Tommy sat staring out the side window.

When they reached the carnival the dirt parking lot was a sea of mud and the grounds were empty except for the brilliantly lit carousel and the cloaked silhouette of Mr. Adams. John led Tommy across the muddy field and stopped to wipe his feet before he stepped onto the polished wood floor of the carousel.

"That will not be necessary," Mr. Adams said above the sound of the rain.

When they climbed aboard the carousel the sound of the rain fell away. Tommy sat on a white bench with carved octopus tentacles wrapping its sides.

"Mr. Roberts, I trust you have brought me your decision?"

"I have."

"Please have a seat," Mr. Adams said pointing at the empty spot next to Tommy.

John sat next to his son.

"Well, then I thank you Mr. Roberts. Tommy, it has been a rare pleasure," Mr. Adams said with a long bow.

Mr. Adams opened the door in the center of the carousel.

"But Mr. Adams what happens now?" John asked. Don't you want my answer?"

"That will not be necessary," Mr. Adams said shutting the door behind him.

The lights of the carousel flickered and went out, leaving John and Tommy in the dark. The carousel began spinning backwards, faster and faster, until the world became a blur and John lost consciousness.

He felt a gentle pat on his shoulder. The morning sun caused mist to rise off the grass of the overgrown field.

"Dad, wake up."

John looked around at the rotted hulk of the carousel. The carved horses had collapsed on shattered legs and water dripped through holes in the roof.

"Dad?"

John turned to find Tommy standing over him, but he was no longer his child-like Tommy Boy. He was a grown man with a wife and two young sons, and enjoyed the life John had always wished for him.

"Dad, you need to stop wandering off like this. You had us scared to death," Tommy said.

Tommy took the keys to the Dodge from John and helped him into his truck.

"Let's get you home and into some warm clothes," Tommy said.

A breeze blew across the overgrown grass as they drove through the field, and the old carousel began to spin.

AUTHOR BIO

WILLIAM MCNALLY is the author of *Four Corners Dark* and is working on his next book *Beneath the Veil*. He lives in Georgia with his wife, Lily, and four rescue dogs.